HAUNTING AND SPIRITUAL STORIES

HAUNTING
AND
SPIRITUAL STORIES

KENNETH G. GARY
HEDY M. GRAY

Ms Gray is a PushCart Literary Award nominee, December 2015

HAUNTING AND SPIRITUAL STORIES

Cover Production by Ean K. Pegram.
Illustrations by Kasim "Guillotine" Gary www.TheKasinoChamp.com

iUniverse books may be ordered through booksellers or by contacting:

iUniverse
1663 Liberty Drive
Bloomington, IN 47403
www.iuniverse.com
1-800-Authors (1-800-288-4677)

ISBN: 978-1-4917-9386-2 (sc)
ISBN: 978-1-4917-9387-9 (e)

Library of Congress Control Number: 2016907198

Print information available on the last page.

iUniverse rev. date: 06/22/2016

DEDICATION

This book is dedicated to Mrs. Mamie Odessa Hale. She was our maternal grandmother and the embodiment of the oral story telling tradition in our family.

With the exception of "The White Dog", none of these are literally her stories. These are a collection of stories created and written by my sister and myself. However, they emanate from grandma's <u>inspiration</u> for story telling.

SPECIAL THANKS TO

Chanel Gray
Zachary Crowder
Gary Hines
Cynthia Gary

COMMENTS ON STORIES IN 'HAUNTING AND SPIRITUAL STORIES'

Wow! This was one of the most complex ghost stories I've ever read. Nothing suddenly jumping out, and yelling, "BOO!". Instead a tale that works on the mind, much like the movie Chinatown. Clues are introduced, taken away, then reintroduced for a conclusion that is more mental than paranormal, showing the horrors that can be found in the human mind. And like Chinatown, this story will need to be read two or three times to gather all the nuances. A true masterpiece of haunting. Not scary—terrifying.

- Lester K. Kloss Jr., Television Producer. From the blog on 'www.themoonlitroad.com' re; "The Spring House Sale", included within this volume.

Loved this story. I never guessed the content which I usually am very good at; this one was one surprise after another. Never guessed the ending which I am very good at. Loved the whole story. From one writer to another....great job!

-Sandra Hender, Author. Comments on 'The Gray House" published at 'www.themoonlitroad.com'. Printed within this volume.

INTRODUCTION

On a daily basis, families both preserve and create traditions: our behavior at mealtimes, games on long family trips, the approach to bedtime for the kids. Our very humanity imbues these seemingly mundane events with life. Thus we participate in the maintenance and creation of culture. Such traditions can coalesce and become institutions. One such institution in our family has been story telling.

Given the above, I have three objectives here:

One objective is a contribution to the legacy of truly haunting tales; the kind that existed before we could resort to a plethora of special effects. The kind of tale that is not easily dismissed at the end of the reading; rather it reverberates, dispersing the gossamer veil of comfort and certainty that surrounds us, heightening our hidden, trembling vulnerability. I for one, shall confess my fears of long dark hallways, and my refusal to retire for the evening in a room with an open door.

The second objective is to elevate the oral tradition of storytelling to more than vestigial status. Those moments spent with the kids just before they go to sleep are ripe with potential today as they were before the explosion of the electronic age. These stories are largely written in storytelling style. They can be read by a Story Teller, tailored to the audience at hand and delivered verbally; typically to children - to make the kids sleep better at night.

This book itself is the third objective, in that it attempts to combine the sentiments above, in print affording an adventure for the reader while equipping the storyteller with material. Or, just for one's reading enjoyment.

While it may appear gruesome to adults, kids do love to be scared. They will beg for it. To that end, I hope these tales equip you, story teller, with enough material to weave, like colored ink in water, burgeoning images that are cast upon the richest stage of all; the vast and vibrant imagination of a child. Besides, a scared child sleeps better.

Tell the story slowly, they will listen better. Use your voice like a matador; in concert with gestures and countenance, it is all a storyteller has. And remember; even though you serve as the conduit for these tales, do not think for one moment, as the creatures within squeeze through from their world into this one thanks to your story telling, that they will not cast a salivating glare upon you as their object of interest…

TABLE OF CONTENTS

Grandma's Tales 1
The Cruise Ship 7
The Grey House 23
Little Lies 35
The Treasure 47
3433 3rd Ave South 61
The Hospital 71
The White Dog 81
The Painting 89
The Spring House Sale 99
One Blue Mitten 111
The Halloween Chase 121

"Grandma's Tales"

By Kenneth G. Gary

Prelude

"There was a certain trance like power to her stories; where did they gain such power from?"

- Any member of her audience

Once upon a time…

When I was a little boy I enjoyed my Grandmothers stories more than anything. Each time, by stories end, I was seized by fear. Soon thereafter, I would eagerly ask for another one. There is no rational explanation for this seeming self - torture, but I could not resist; and I was not alone.

My siblings and I would often scramble, like a litter of puppies, to gather around Grandma's chair when story-time commenced. It was always a bit of a wrestling match to find a seat both comfortable and safe as possible. Then, the story would begin…

On those occasions the best position was sitting at her feet with my back pressed against her shins - in order to see whatever may be coming…

In the dining room, it could be in the middle of the day; and still, once the story began, the temperature would change, the walls themselves would dissolve into scenery weaved by her word; something in me knew even then that these were not *just* stories.

The fear her stories engendered was palpable. There was no question that it was actually happening as she spoke. And I would cling to every terror-laden word.

At times the mesmerizing effect of her stories would linger, like a faint color, a tingling sensation. It made me wonder if others could affect an audience the same way. I noticed that the principal's speech in the auditorium at my older brothers graduation, the Broadcasters of great sports events, even the president's state of the union speech-- none of these deliveries evinced the captivating qualities of her stories.

Grandma had prominent cheekbones, long, mostly gray hair usually rolled into a bun in back, a somewhat sharp nose and a somewhat sharp personality to go with it. She walked stooped over a bit aided by a walking stick, which had a short ninety-degree branch at the top, which served as a handle. She wielded this instrument with expertise rivaling any combatant, often to my younger brothers chagrin.

One morning, I was in the kitchen with Grandma. I was eating oatmeal she had just prepared. I was the first one up that morning so I felt lucky to have first choice of everything. All of a sudden, unbidden and for no discernable reason she said to me "I just saw my dead husband standing by the stove. Still all dressed up. I said to him '*What are you doing here? You know you aint supposed to be here.*'" Then she said he turned around and walked through the wall.

What?! Where is he now? my mind screamed. Is it safe to go into the next room? And who can just command a ghost to go away?

The breadth of her powers multiplied in my mind.

As time progressed, Grandma eventually declined, as all people do towards the very end of life; first into a sedentary existence, followed by a semi conscious state where clarity surfaced only once every several days. No one else ever seemed to know, and I was not trying to share the information with anyone, but I could get her to tell me a story even when she was not in a totally clear state of mind.

In fact, when I slipped into Grandma's closed room and requested a story, Grandma would move with a mechanical effortlessness, as if by strings attached, into a half sitting position on one elbow, and begin the tale…

Finally, the only time she was visited by lucidity at all was when I requested a story. Moreover, her tales began to take on theatrical proportions far--exceeding their former expressions. There were fluctuations in her voice that vividly painted the soul of every character; a narrative magic that sent one's mind hurtling through the heavens, and a sense of gravity that took one straight to Hades at her merest whim.

These stories bent the fabric of the universe itself. They became unbearably frightful.

One day, with considerable trepidation, I made a request, and there was no response. I knew immediately that a certain vitality had gone, never to return. Soon after, with no more stories, Grandma passed away.

The wake was in the evening. Actually, it ended up being at night because so many were traveling from afar. The entire event took place in a fairly modest church. There were many rows of pews; there must have been twenty at least; hard, slippery wooden benches are what they really were. And there was an aisle between them stretching from the pulpit to the church entrance. And it was hot that day.

The preacher who delivered the eulogy was adorned with an exquisite long black robe and spoke from the pulpit. As a child, I could not help thinking of it as a stage since the area was raised and required climbing several stairs to gain access. There were gracious flower arrangements populating the 'stage', and there was a magnificent statue of Jesus on the cross at the back of it all.

In the middle of the floor, in front of the stage, was an ominous rectangular container, which I knew contained my grandmother.

It was a dreadfully long service. There is something about those occasions where people get a chance at the microphone and they seem to never want to stop -- as if this is the only sunshine they will ever get.

Finally, after an interminable parade of events, the service ended and the only remaining formality was to line up in the aisle, visit the casket, and do whatever it is that people do when that time comes. Some people talk to the corpse, some cry, some are too horrified to do anything but submit to the procession, anxiously hoping for the dreadful event to end.

What caught my eye, however, was that there seemed to be far more people visiting the casket than had participated in the overall funeral proceedings.

I do not know if it was the tears in my eyes, for I did cry for my dear Grandmothers departure, or just the effusive display of emotions from everyone, but there were people there that I did not even remotely recognize. Well, I guess this occurs at funerals; they bring us all together at least for the event.

As the line I was in slowly progressed, allowing each to wince or cry as he or she pleased, I could not but notice that the population within the room was still increasing beyond reasonable measure. Many of them were only lining the walls of the room, out of the light so that their faces really could not be made out at all. While nearly everyone was wearing black, they were wearing a very dark gray; the color of shadows. And, there was a distinct 'something', a presence of some kind, emanating from them. And it increased as I approached the casket.

I began to feel that old tingling feeling again. The feeling that would linger after one of Grandma's stories. I wondered *why would I feel this now…*

Upon reaching the casket, I changed my mind. Stop! Why did I ever ask for all those stories in the first place…I do not want to see

Grandma anymore, I do not want her to be dead either, why am I here!

Realizing that no one would understand if I fled from the room in terror, I caught hold of myself and peered into the casket. Grandma looked innocuous enough. She did not move (*had I thought that she might*?), her eyes did not open...but I perceived that I was surrounded by those 'people', which had been standing around the edges of the room. Suddenly they were all standing around me at the casket. And still, even close up: they were shadow colored, and had no faces!

It was then that I realized no one else could see them. Well, what is at the far extreme of terror itself? Death. I simply froze and gave up my own existence. There was nowhere to run. Only Grandma could chase away ghosts anyway! She told me so!

Then I could hear my Grandmothers voice- "Don't be afraid, child, they have always been around you. You have always known that my tales were no ordinary stories. That is because *they* have always taken turns talking to you through me."

I looked at her. She was dead. No movement, no warmth, no nothing. These spirits were accustomed to using her voice.

"It will be uncomfortable at first, with them struggling with one another to spin the tale this way or that. But as time passes, you will learn to balance yourself, and let them join you in becoming the next storyteller of this family. They actually cannot do it without you. But you certainly do not want to deny them, either."

"Above all, remember to always tell tales of terror, or they will become rancorous and agitated, and they may even visit their horror upon you if you do not!"

I wanted to fall to my knees and just cry. I wanted to jump into the casket with her, beg her to make it stop, because, who else would believe such an event if I should explain it to them. I should have told someone long ago about the very special nature of Grandma and her stories; but I was too selfish, and kept it all to myself. Now it, and all of 'them', really would be kept to me alone. For the rest of my life, until someone, who likes my stories a great deal, visits me in my casket...

THE END

Epilog

For those who hunger for explanations, many people in the town at that time suggested that the deep well at the edge of my Grandmothers property carried water, and souls, from the hills in the west where the US Army massacred an entire Indian tribe during the war many years ago. This was supposed to be the origin of the spirits that surrounded Grandma.

Others insisted that the hills in the East had been the place of a long established coven of witches, whose worst thoughts and remnants of the cauldrons they boiled found their way into the well used by my Grandmother.

All I really know now is that I will have to live with *them*, wherever they are from. Every morning when I wake; they are there, waiting; they do not sleep. I often hear them clashing for no discernable reason while I drive to work. At some times during the year, they seem to all retreat in unison, to the distant corners of the universe of my soul. Only to return with replenished vigor, and burning potential for telling their story!

And I always have that tingling feeling.

"The Cruise Ship"

By Kenneth G. Gary

"Not me! Not at any cost; I will not go to prison!"

– Anonymous criminal determined
not to face retribution.

Once upon a time…

This was to be the most wondrous of vacations. The sky was an unbelievable blue, this water …this must be an ocean more pure, clearer than most waters could ever aspire to, it revealed everything down to the colored spots on the tropical fish meandering leisurely below.

The tropical breeze was 'hold onto your hat' strong; but it was pleasant. The entire scene evoked such vast feelings of freedom; this was one vacation that promised to exceed the claims of the advertisements!

Ahman and Celeste, married for forty plus years, both felt this to be a rejuvenation ordered up by destiny itself. Life goes too fast, children require too much; how immensely fortunate they were – and, in a manner that was utterly uncommon, how deeply this fortune was acknowledged by both though completely unspoken between them. We are so very adept at not appreciating; this is a condition which runs rampant throughout humanity, but this old couple, were you to see them on deck just enjoying (perhaps worshiping) nature's bounty, your pace would slow and your mind would become still as if there were something palpable exuding from the simple peace they shared.

They reclined in lounge chairs near the left rear of the boat, far from the crowds playing games and music. They were near the railing separating them from the boundless ocean where the refreshing salinity could actually reach them. The sparkling white deck, brilliant water and faultless blue sky conspire to produce a stunning scene.

Ahman, enjoying the breeze that his loose fitting Hawaiian shirt afforded him thought; *Celeste is right. Silk is the best fabric. But, Celeste is always right, even when she's wrong.* The years had been kind to him, physically. He was still slim, and in this constant sun his already deep brown skin was beginning to nearly shine.

Ahman rose to retrieve a novel he had been reading, from their cabin. Of course, Celeste, peering over the top of her opaque sunglasses, immediately conjured up several items she too wanted from the cabin, in addition to four principles of re-arrangement he should address 'since you are going to the cabin anyway'.

Celeste too had weathered the years well. She endeavored to secure health with nutritional supplements and maintain her golden skin with oils and such. She wore a very light silk shawl over her bathing suit, as some degree of modesty would demand. Underneath that she wore a body nearly the same as the day they were married.

Without the slightest degradation of mood, Ahman simply complied, feigning genuine interest and understanding, turned to proceed the length of the cruise ship to perform the duties thus suddenly assigned, in their cabin.

With his attention diverted, his stylish white straw hat was swiftly removed from his head and raced overboard like a bird towards the sky. With the speed of the luxury liner, and the wind racing the other direction, his hat was virtually snatched from his head and, once aloft, soared upwards, straight away, like a helium filled balloon – completely free of gravity, until it was simply out of sight.

This event did occasion mild chagrin from Ahman. The hat had been secured at the cost of a lengthy bartering session in which his wife simply would not yield, if it cost all afternoon. This was accomplished while they were lying on the beach at one of the stops the ocean liner scheduled. Since he did not plan to engage in much activity of this sort, Ahman did not realize until this moment that the hat had secretly, unconsciously, become what was to be his souvenir of this vacation.

Over the years Ahman had developed a place in his mind; a place where he could go in any storm, any turmoil, and nearly any onslaught of circumstantial negativity, which prevented his soul from suffering the prevailing infection. But he felt a genuine loss; which signaled an attachment, which was somewhat contrary to the methods he had employed all his life in order to retain an internal freedom in any circumstance.

At the very fringe of his soul he actually felt a distant encroachment of a tumultuous storm; the weather he could see surrounding him was gorgeous, but he felt this storm nevertheless. This storm seemed to carry a deep, reverberating evil song within it...When Celeste, offering one of those comments that hurt more than help, sputtered "Why did you let your hat go!!??". Ahman did not respond, but did catch himself glaring at her, but, with perfect repose, he gathered himself, smiled, and proceeded across the deck to the cabin.

And that was the first time he heard it, close to his ear... "I need your help...". He turned quickly to his left, as that was where the voice seemed to come from, but there was no one there. There was no one near at all. But he had heard it quite clearly, although it sounded like someone driving by in a fast vehicle, where the voice rises and fades as the vehicle travels by.

For long moments he stood there, turning slowly in a circle as if there must have been someone nearby, or someone who would be recognized as the speaker of these words. But there was no one. There were plenty of people on the boat, playing shuffleboard, some sort of bowling game, other activities, but no one close enough to have been responsible for what he had heard.

At a certain point, we become friends to the passage of time, and 'old age' becomes the answer to everything. Besides: the sun, the margaritas and the motion of the boat could all easily contrive to produce illusions of sorts. And, this is vacation; Ahman quickly overlooked the illusion and continued to the cabin to get his novel.

All his life he had loved the sun; and it felt like today's sun would never end, just like it feels in childhood.

Ahman stopped at one of the little makeshift bar huts on his way through the more crowded section of the deck. He ordered a margarita, with no salt. The bartender, as bartenders are prone to do, just began talking with his heavy Jamaican accent; 'Tings come and tings go, sir. But some tings seem to just stay.' Just then, Ahman caught a quick glimpse of several people through the back window of the hut. They appeared to be huddled quite close together, and somehow, the area around them seemed quite dark, unlike the rest of the brightly lit deck.

With some degree of alarm, after finishing the drink preparation the bartender seemed to slam the drink on the counter with thunderous reverberation. At least, it sounded so to Ahman. 'Soon we be leavin' deese troubled waters behind, sir. We will be settin' sail again very soon.' Upon returning his attention to the window at the back of the bar hut, there were no people there and it was just as sunny in the window as it was all over the deck, and indeed, as far as the eye could see.

Drink in hand; Ahman proceeded to their cabin.

Ahman entered their cabin, having completely forgotten the tasks Celeste had assigned, and set out to retrieve the novel he was reading. It was not in the suitcase, nor on the nightstand by the bed, which is where he actually expected it to be. Finally, he sat down in one of the only two chairs in the small cabin, only to find that there apparently was a small pool of water in it, which he had not noticed. Now his pants were wet.

He got up, rummaged through his luggage and found another pair of shorts, dry ones, and he proceeded to change. Putting his first leg through the pants nearly sent him sprawling to the floor because the floor of the cabin was inexplicably wet. He caught his balance enough to change his pants, and continued the search for his novel.

He went into the bathroom, '*may as well, before the long walk back to the sun deck*', and his novel was there on the sink. As he reached to pick it up he heard a distinct clanking sound. Must be someone at the cabin door trying to insert the wrong key into his door.

Ahman went to the door, looked through the peephole, seeing no one, he opened the door to find not only no one, but no one the entire length of the hall in either direction. The hall was of prodigious length, so much so that no one could have been at the door making the sound and now be out of sight down the hall in either direction. But, maybe they entered one of the other cabins along the way; that would explain it. It would have had to be a very quick entry if that were the case.

Before this last thought had even settled in his mind, he heard the clanking noise again: from behind him, *inside* his cabin. Ahman swung around to see…nothing. There was nothing there.

Well. I have my novel now, and at this point, I am going back into the sunlight. At that moment, he heard it again, very faintly; 'I need your help!'

Unperturbed, Ahman left the cabin, locked the door and before he had taken ten steps he was completely back in relaxation mode, thinking about the sunshine above on the deck.

'Where are my magazines!??' insisted Celeste.

Ahman had no recollection of such a request – if indeed it was made at all. But this was vacation. After all, he calculated that returning to fetch her magazines, which would then occupy her attention, a superior option to refusal, and suffering her endless capacity for complaint.

Ahman again walked the length of the deck, admiring the way the deep blue of the sky made the fluffy white clouds look like they were material enough to lounge upon.

Once in the cabin, Ahman did know exactly which magazines she had been engulfed in lately. He bent over to collect them from her carry on bag by the bed. Upon rising and turning around he was utterly shocked to find himself literally face to face with a black man, barely clothed at all, and dripping wet. Ahman gasped at the suddenness of this encounter, but before he could utter a sound the man was gone. He did not leave; he simply disappeared.

Ahman did not know what to think; for several moments, he had no thoughts at all.

However, he did begin to recollect what he had 'seen'. The mind has an amazing photographic capacity that lends itself to later analysis. The 'vision' or 'apparition' was only there for the blink of an eye, but, upon reflection, there was no question that the man was dismally dressed, evinced a clear history of dejection, and had a searing appeal in his eyes. In addition to being soaking wet.

Looking down, there was indeed a pool of water on the floor where the man had been standing.

This is one of the problems with taking a cruise, he thought. If we were at home, at this moment I would collect my wife and simply leave town, taking nothing. But you cannot just leave a cruise ship, can you?

In fact, Ahman again collected the magazines, which had fallen to the floor – this time without diverting his vision from the surrounding room. He then carefully made his way around the wet spot on the floor, eyes sweeping the cabin in front and behind him (as far as this is possible), until he finally ended up backing out of the cabin into the hallway.

At the far end of the hall, approaching him was a gentlemen exquisitely attired in a loose fitting white suit that was very nearly highly stereotyped sea faring garb of the very rich. As they approached one another, the strangers smile was very nearly luminous, and skin that had an inner radiance to it. His manner was utterly seductive and comfortable. They talked for several minutes, and, without remembering much, Ahman only recalled as he returned to the deck, that he had invited the young gentleman to dine with them that evening.

Ahman also knew they were to wear their 'best attire' for the occasion.

Any occasion to dress formally was not lost on Celeste, and she hummed a tune as she adorned herself for the evening. Ahman had a mild foreboding within his heart. He could feel currents within himself, as deep as beneath this ocean liner that felt fatal and final. And he could not forget the barely dressed man he had seen in his cabin.

Ahman wore white linen pants and shirt. Celeste donned a long silk flowered dress that was utterly flattering to her youthful body.

At their short rectangular table, where each of them sat at one of the more distal ends, with the third side snuggled against the ships railing over the water, as Ahman and Celeste toasted one another with champagne, almost magically, the young stranger joined them; they had not noticed his approach. Instantly another glass was ordered, delivered, and Celeste poured 'him' a glass, after which they all toasted to 'life'.

Ahman had a brief thought that he did not even know this gentleman's name, and Celeste, the most inquisitive of all beings, did not inquire either. They simply acted as though they all knew one another, and that this was a planned event.

As they enjoyed what seemed to be silence, it became apparent that it was actually preparation. The ambiance changed color entirely when the waiter returned to the table, and upon setting about the removal of the third arrangement of silverware from the middle of the table, he reached, effortlessly, directly through the young guest as though he were made of smoke, to retrieve the silverware.

Ahman glanced at Celeste, with all the silent communication that only an aged couple can have. She too, had recognized that fate was indeed dining with them. Their Guest was immaterial – yet he was indeed 'here'. The waiter dutifully collected the third place setting from the table and departed.

"Who are you, sir?" inquired Ahman.

"My name would roar in your ears like a thousand horns. No need for names." responded their guest.

"What can we do for you?" queried Celeste, with utmost concern, and an amazing lack of fear.

"I have a story to tell you, and a favor to ask of you. Let us begin with the story..."

Celeste leaned back in her chair, relaxed. Ahman did the same, with his arms on the armrest of the chair. They both found their eyes not closed, but drifting in a non-focused fashion.

The 'story' was conveyed in images; no words were involved. They could see, no, they could feel an old 19th century cargo ship thrashing about in a relentless storm as sometimes abducts the Caribbean seas. There was a man, clearly in control, undoubtedly the captain, who was storming too and fro more than the weather itself. He shouted and struck the others in the crew if they did not immediately follow his instructions, as impossible as they may be, for the storm was completely overwhelming to any mortal adjustment whatsoever.

This captain wore knee high leather boots, a hat so weathered as to nearly have no shape at all, an ancient double-breasted military type coat with a sword and pistol at his waist.

His ship was being pursued by two other ships. Unfortunately for him, he was a known criminal and these ships had laid in wait for his return to the Caribbean Sea, where once and for all they would exact the price upon him that he deserved.

Captain Fein, had for all of his adult life, pursued riches and fame. He did so to maniacal extremes. It had become increasingly difficult for him to secure participants on his voyages as time went on.

As the English ships closed in on him, Captain Fein became obsessed with a fury seldom known to man. Slavery had been outlawed for over a decade, but it was the Captains only known trade and expertise; he could drive a crew of sailors and subdue 450 slaves from West Africa to the New World with regularity. He knew nothing else and felt no remorse for over 30 years. And, though illegal, this was to be his last trip. The final effort to 'cash in' on his expertise – and this time he would not squander the reward.

Suddenly, what the Captain thought was only two ships, turned out to be even more. Not only was he being chased from behind, but even through the driving rain he could see that he was cut off from the front also.

As if fed by the very storm itself, Captain Fein's unreasonable rage erupted beyond all bounds. With lightning for a background, he drew his saber; continuously slashing at the ships railing as he stormed about, and injuring several crew members that simply happened to be nearby.

The dark skies unleashed a rumbling roar of thunder that must have collected over eons to account for such ferocity. At that moment, Captain Fein knew with complete clarity what he must do. His capture was now inevitable as he was completely contained by English ships before and behind in addition to land on both sides. But, there is no crime if there is no bounty. He allowed himself an unstifled roar of laughter at this: how much more clever he was than those who pursue him!

Captain Fein looked skyward, triumphantly, as he had resolved to address all issues, but, questioningly almost as if he had heard something from somewhere other than this earthly plane.

On the cruise ship, with clear skies and an extraordinary sunset, their guest evinced an air of emergency, and, eyes shining with electricity, he exclaimed:

"I need your help. They need your help. This opportunity arises only on rare occasions and time is upon us. We have the chance to alleviate the damnable suffering of hundreds, if we are only willing to make the sacrifice!"

Ahman: "What is this suffering you speak of, and, who is it that suffers?"

Celeste: "Who are you?"

Stranger: "I am what you might call an Angel. And the answer to whom it is that suffers lies in the remainder of my story."

With that statement, both Ahman and Celeste were returned to their vision of the intractable storm; storms both climatic and behavioral, upon the ship of Captain Fein. With nearly regular frequency, you could hear the howls of a crewman as he was swept overboard, knowing that he would never be saved, and that Captain Fein would not even consider an attempt at retrieval.

You could see the mounting detachment in the eyes of Captain Fein. They were so wide as to reflect the limits of the horizon, and yet see nothing on board in his immediate vicinity. The Captain had gone mad.

But madness has its talents. While surrounded by black, vicious and stormy waters, the Captain could 'hear' that there was a plot afoot in the heavens to thwart his plan. But he would not be deterred; he would not be apprehended with a ship full of slaves years after the transport of slaves had become illegal.

Captain Fein ordered that the slaves be brought on deck. A sailor very near him immediately recognized the problem that would be introduced. Upon objecting to his Captain, his head was immediately removed with the saber.

No one else objected. No matter how much it promised to complicate matters with this raging storm, the slaves below were all marched onto deck. The clanking of their chains could somehow be heard even above the prolific storm that would not abate.

Angel: "I am counting on your strength to continue pursuit of this story." Ahman and Celeste could hear the Angel as if from very far away, but quite clearly through the ancient storm, which they could still see.

And they emerged; endless streams of them: hundreds. They were clearly ancient, all in several lines because they were chained together, to a long chain that ran between them. The captain of their vessel, was about to be apprehended on the high seas with a huge cargo of slaves after slavery had been abolished in the new world. In his madness, he ordered that the ships anchor be attached to the end of their chain and thrown overboard, before the English ships could overtake him and first punish him for breaking the law, and, second, steal his 'cargo'.

When the anchor hit the water, the main chain dived deeply with it; and panic stricken Africans immediately began their inexorable, mortal dive to the bottom of the Atlantic. The screams welled up into an orchestra of terror, for there was no escape. Real horror is when it can be seen but not escaped.

Men, women and children, were all helplessly plunged into the abysmal sea; with no hope, no recourse. Even those at the end, who could anticipate their fate in time to latch onto some stable structure, found the sheer weight and momentum far too much for anyone to resist. All were taken to the bottom.

These were the souls that tread the halls of the great and luxurious ocean liner passing above their unsanctified graves. They bore no genuine horror for the guests; not intentional, nor could they move on given the sudden and criminal nature of their demise. People may die in automobile accidents without warning; but they are just that: accidents. And they are attended to by those entities that are 'on duty' at the time. But very often, people who are intentionally killed, without provocation, without reason, with full malice and particularly en mass; these souls cannot all be retrieved in time: the window closes. And they fail to pass over.

It is exceedingly rare, but, sometimes the angels are stricken with such grief that they miss the 'window' in time where souls must be retrieved...for while they themselves are timeless, all mortal beings, dead or alive, are time bound. Even Angels cannot alter these formulae. Imagine entering a blazing wall of flames; that is how Angels experience human suffering – far more acutely than any mortal can. And it is dreadfully painful.

Ahman: "Why are you showing this to us?"

Celeste simply grasped Ahman's hand across the table with a knowing conviction.

The Angel saw this, leaned back in his chair waiting for Celeste to reveal what he knew she was aware of.

Celeste "You were the one who could not garner all those souls that night. Weren't you."

Angel "Yes".

Celeste "And you need our help to open the door again, to complete your task."

Angel "Yes".

Ahman was amazed at the sagacity Celeste displayed. Though staunchly religious, she had never exhibited any clairvoyant tendencies, belief or even interest in such things. Now, here she was, completely awash with what seemed to be preternatural capacities.

Ahman "What do you mean by 'open the door again'", he was asking both Celeste and the Angel.

Celeste "He wants us to die. It is the only way the door is opened; it is the door of mortality."

Their discussion continued for some time.

This 'Angel' was asking him to give up his life in order to create a doorway to lead the others to their proper resting place. The Angel could not just abduct whomever he wanted at whatever time. The scheme of things imposed limits on Angels too. This condition had been over a hundred and fifty years in preparation; the Angel needed a soul wide enough to create momentum that would draw the others through to the place they needed to be.

But the Angel was not only asking Ahman. He needed Celeste too. Together they could, if they would give up their lives, create the necessary condition for the Angel to pull them through along with all the others that had suffered so unnecessarily for so long. And it had to be tonight.

Lastly, the Angel could not kill a human; not directly. But he could accurately detect the recurrence of certain conditions.

At this moment the 'Angel' pointed over the edge of the ship to the water and moved his finger in a slow circular pattern. Ahman and Celeste understood to look in the direction he was pointing. They could see a small whirlpool in the midst of utterly calm water. There was a small glowing light at the far end of the whirlpool.

The Angel grabbed an orange from the fruit bowl on their table and tossed it directly onto the edge of the whirlpool, where it immediately began to traverse the edge, passing the strange light on each revolution. Each time it did, the light was refracted into a nearly blinding orange glow with rays that spread out to what seemed to be eternity.

Angel "Not all of time is straight. Sometimes it goes in circles. These are rare conditions but they occur sometimes when extraordinary events take place. We have the opportunity to pass the light just as you see in the whirlpool. Tonight."

This task however required their consent; their sacrifice. The final circumstance necessary was for both Ahman and Celeste to experience the original tragedy. They had to chain themselves to the center chain holding all the others, and follow them into death.

Celeste spoke up, and insisted that she would do this, if the children could be spared. But, the Angel replied that they were already dead; no bodies available for their souls, nothing he could do. Celeste insisted that he at least pray, at least for the children to be spared. The Angel agreed, knowing it to be in vain.

Ahman "What children do you speak of?"

Angel, surprised "You did not tell him, did you."

Celeste "No, I did not know how."

Angel "Ahman, she saw the children from the ship, well, their souls anyways, walking down the corridor towards her last night. Just as you saw one of the men from the slave ship earlier this afternoon."

Celeste had seen silhouettes of these children long before this voyage began. In her dreams, she had seen them in straight lines or in circles, but always close together. The vision would begin with them playing but end with their violent removal from her view, accompanied by screams of absolute terror.

Ahman "And just why could this task not be completed when it occurred. Why must our lives be involved?"

At this the Angel brought his hands from underneath the table and thrust them forth, palms down, for Ahman and Celeste to view. They were charred, burned and cracked. There were still glowing embers visible underneath the cracked and curled sections of what used to be skin. This Angel had nearly forsaken his own existence in his effort to gather and guide the departing souls, but the sheer burning pain had overcome him, and he too had been suffering all these years; the doors of mortality had literally closed upon him in the midst of his efforts.

Celeste gave the Angel a look of resolution that he could not quite fathom. There was an unmistakable portentous element in her countenance. It was resolve. She now understood the dreams she had experienced. She knew why she was on this ship, in these waters, at this time.

The Angel thought that, amazingly, she knew even more. Uncharacteristically, with a touch of desperation, and contrary to his covenant, the Angel revealed "I was directed to you, by someone that you know…".

For long moments Ahman and Celeste looked deeply within each other's eyes.

Celeste: "Could I speak with my husband alone, please?"

Angel, with utter respect, and divine remorse: "Yes. Please, I must implore you to be mindful of time."

The Angel stood up, turned away from the table, and in the space of three paces he was simply 'gone'.

Ahman: "This is beyond unbelievable, this…is…"

Celeste: "This is where we are."

Being together this long, each knows the others 'buttons' of sensitivity. They very nearly fell into this valley out of sheer habit as emotions were running high, but the gravity of the situation prevailed, and descending into argument was not a realistic threat.

Celeste, imploringly: "Ahman, I saw them. They were only children. I could even feel the pain of their plight, being utterly lost, and completely aware of it. The tragedy he showed us still fresh in their minds – and all this time!"

Ahman, seeing where this was going: "And what of our daughter, Nimosha? And her two children? Do we not have a duty in that direction, one that is solely ours?"

Celeste: "Nimosha and Hassan will be fine. They are obviously doing a great job with their children already. And what of the hundreds of souls that both you and I are aware of? What of them? When will the light he showed us be approached again?"

Ahman:" I don't know...how can he ask such a thing in the first place? I do not believe this is happening!"

Celeste: "You know it is happening. And, the question is; how does one walk away? Could you live with that?"

Reaching that plateau, the tears began to flow down Celeste' face. Ahman too was beginning to yield to convulsive abdominal sobs. Ahman got up, walked around the table to Celeste' chair and bent down on one knee (his good knee). He folded his arms on the armrest of her chair and her arm encircled his neck. His head down in her lap, and the heretofore-tearless Ahman began to cry.

Celeste looked out over the great ocean and thought about her mother. A human rights pioneer before the advent of mass communication; when the world was *not* watching, and such activity at this time demanded a courage that rarely walks the earth. There were endless testimonies to her mothers' bravery, resolution and determination at her funeral. Celeste could not help but feel that her mother was watching now.

She remembered how, even though her family was of substantial means, they were taught lessons of value and humility at every opportunity. There was one Christmas where a not-so-close family of relatives had suffered a serious fire in their home. Celeste' parents not only sent them substantial support, they also involved Celeste and her siblings by not having Xmas gifts that year in recognition of their relative's plight, thus allowing them to send more, and allowing their children to share in the sacrifice.

Celeste learned the meaning of sacrifice early and often in life. She willingly accompanied her mother on missions of mercy and developed a genuine ardent desire to 'serve'. Ahman often accused her of abandoning logic, but Celeste felt that it was not logic which would prevail in the larger scheme of things anyway. Celeste had made her mind up. And she knew that neither of them could walk away. That was the pivot upon which her thoughts anchored; not whether you could do something, but whether you could live with *not d*oing it.

She also now knew who had directed this Angel to her.

Ahman rose from his kneeling position, eyes now dry, and returned to his chair. They continued to talk. The waiter constantly refreshed their meaningless drinks with absolute attention. It appeared so inconsequential as to be nearly humorous to Ahman – 'if he only knew' Ahman thought.

The Angel, unbidden, returned. He had no choice but to be scrupulous about time at this point. He said nothing. His eyes said everything.

This time Ahman noticed the difference. Before he could gather the words to form his question the Angel revealed: "Yes, I have an effect upon people by my very presence. I do not influence them or their decisions, but I do calm souls. You have no idea of the tumult the immediately departed can experience. It is a necessary quality for my task."

Having made her decision some time ago Celeste stood up, Ahman followed, and they embraced one final time. Then, with the Angel between them, holding their hands (the scars he revealed were now repressed – and his hands were certainly material enough, even warm), the three of them simply walked towards the front of the deck of the ocean liner until they emerged, unheralded, upon the deck of the 18th cargo ship. Day turned to night in the midst of a storm that had to be inspired by hell itself.

Instantly, captain Fein's antennae shrieked with alarm. Not only was (so called) heaven out to disparage his plans, but they were here now! Somewhere! Even this fateful, vengeful storm could not mask their proximity. The captain, given the extremity of his evil, was attracting insight and support from hell itself.

Captain Fein raced to and fro, killing several crew, several slaves, and simply striking out wildly because he had no idea where the intrusion to his plans was coming from. But he would not be denied. He knew 'they' were here this time!

Fighting the immense intensity of the storm, the Angel guided Ahman and Celeste into the midst of the chained slaves, only moments before the fateful instant where they were all attached to the ships anchor. Without drawing any attention whatsoever (as their fine evening attire had transformed into filthy rags as were worn by all the others), the Angel saw to it they were attached with shackles to the main chain, which now had the ships anchor at the end of it. Even this prodigious storm could not stifle the odor of human waste and despair.

One of the crew cried out, feeling the eternal damnation of such an act. He was immediately slaughtered by the captain. The anchor was secured, and the scene was replayed exactly as before, with the addition of Ahman and Celeste being present.

However, before the anchor was thrust into the water, Celeste noticed that there was not just one main chain to which everyone was connected. There were at least two tributaries, one of which had at least 70 children attached to it. And, thank God for hairpins! She removed it from her mouth…

This time, Captain Fein, in his fervor to insure his plans were not thwarted, stumbled into the midst of the slaves as they began to careen overboard. His leg became hopelessly entangled in the chains and he too was sent plummeting to his death, as if to open a balancing doorway in another direction…and the horror repeated itself to conclusion, for the last time.

On the news that evening, it was reported that seventy-three naked, black, children were found washed upon shore in South Florida. No one knew who they were. They did not speak English. The children were healthy, but very, very hungry.

Some had shackles with broken chains on their wrists.

The End.

"The Grey House"

By Kenneth G. Gary

Prelude

"I know that old woman in that huge, crumbling, gray house is hiding a secret, a dead body, *something*. I just know it!"

– words of an anonymous woman
in the neighborhood.

Once upon a time…

When I was a young boy we played any number of sports and games outside in all areas of our neighborhood. The entire area was our domain; with one unacknowledged exception.

It was not something that we talked about openly, unless it was Halloween, but there was one very large, decayed, gray house at the end of our 'territory' that, collectively, we instinctively avoided.

The house sat at the end of a cul de sac, making this street a prime candidate for us to play on.

We had in the past, heard of the terror of attempting to retrieve an errant baseball from the front yard. Currently there was no particular event associated with this perception; just a feeling. This alone was enough to make us realize that the air within that yard was forbidding. In fact, there are a number of prize balls of all sorts in that yard that were simply never recovered. It could even be the ninth inning, sun setting, mothers calling; but whenever the ball fell into that yard, it was the unspoken termination of whatever series was underway. Silently, no boasting, no arguments; the game just dissolved.

It was the kind of house that you just did not turn and walk away from; you tended to look over your shoulder for an extended portion of your departure. There was a subterranean concern with having 'disturbed' whatever lay within…there was a '*please do not follow me home*' thought in the mind of anyone who in any way encroached.

That year, the hometown team made it to the super bowl. In those days, we were so adept at sneaking into any stadium that our only concern was getting enough cash for hot dogs and pop. This we accomplished also. With the game being local, we basically had fortune not merely smile upon us but bursting with a cornucopia of joy.

When our team won, underneath the bleachers, and everywhere else, people celebrated without restraint. One particularly exuberant (*drunk*) man pulled me aside and pushed a real NFL labeled football into my stomach, just like a hand off. "Here's a souvenir, kid" he mumbled.

Well, to me at that age, I thought it was the game ball! I ran before he could change his clouded mind. Showing my friends, they immediately wanted to go out to our street, and play a game with this wonderful ball that *found its way* into our lives.

With the seemingly limitless energy of youth, when legs just wanted to run of their own accord, we played and played up and down the avenue that night. The ball seemed to bring some magic to the game because there were more extraordinary plays performed than ever before. Finally, there was one long sideline pass that ended up too close to the fence, and even though I tipped it with my left hand, it did not bounce into receiving range, and it went over (it was 'sucked' over) the fence.

It went over the fence into the yard of the big gray house.

Typically, we would all simply subdue (or be subdued) our impulses and quietly go home for the evening. But this was a special ball, and the super bowl had filled us with emotions that made us feel it was the game of our lives. This ball had to be retrieved.

I immediately drafted Bruce and Ronnie as my co-agents in what I had already determined to be a rescue mission. We lost a lot of balls before; we are not losing this one. Neither of them objected, as they were both intoxicated by the day, the super bowl and the ball. We approached the fence to figure a plan of retrieval. Behind us, out of view, everyone else slowly backed up, with that same mesmerized expression, and finally simply turned away and went home.

What came to mind with the force of thunder was the recollection that only two people had ever entered this yard before. One, a high school football star, who instantly broke his leg after climbing the fence, and, his arm upon breaking his fall. The other incident involved a very popular boy that must have incurred an even more horrific fate as no one would even tell us what had taken place. We were 'too young'. All we could gather was that the grief-stricken, morose expressions on the faces of his friends that day spelled certain doom. We never saw him again.

No matter. The ball is outside in the yard. It cannot have gone too close to the house. Besides conquering the prodigious undergrowth, what really in this world of sunshine and blue sky could stop us?

We were terrified.

The fence was chest high, for all three of us. But the vines and bushes that were never cut, caused one to forcibly dig through them in order to get a clear view of the yard even on top of the old wooden fence. And these vines and other undergrowth were tenacious; at points it seemed they grew straight through un-cracked areas in the wood itself.

Assessing the landscape we decided to try to first make visual contact with the ball. Then we could decide a plan of action that would most likely secure our lives in this mission and return us safely to this side of the fence. After a visual search, we could not see the ball. However, we remained undaunted.

Unnoticed, we transformed into a band of predators that surveyed the African Savannah. With unspoken stealth, we found an area that permitted the easiest access thru the brush, vines, and over the fence.

There was a movement in one of the upstairs windows…*not now; did it notice me? don't look!* Let us just get the ball; that's all. In that strange way that people will expect that if they do not look directly at the car as they cross in front of, it will, by some unwritten law, not hit them. Just don't look!

We had no real idea how large this cul de sac property really was. The house, easily observed from a distance down the street, was in reality thirty yards from the fence, and much taller, wider and far more decrepit than anyone ever suspected. And the gray color was not so much a color as it was the complete absence of any color at all. It was the color left when absolutely all other color is washed away. And it was unsettling. The house just looked dead.

The house had a broad porch in front spanning the width of the house raised by just a few stairs height in the middle. On each side there appeared to be about three vertical support poles holding the overhanging roof above. The second floor was about like the first with four large windows across. And there was the peaked attic above, with two windows.

Ronnie had received several cuts in the effort. One, on the back of his right hand, which probably deserved some attention, but before we knew it Ronnie licked it several times, applying saliva and clearing the blood. He looked up at us and whispered "It's okay".

Crouching to a height just above the never tended sea of weeds covering the yard; we spread out to better locate our target in minimum time. We were far enough apart to expand the swath of the search, and close enough to not leave unexplored areas in between us.

Spread out, as we were, me in the middle, Bruce on my far left and Ronnie on my far right, we hesitantly began to search through, what seemed to be all the wheat in Kansas, for the ball.

Unbelievably, I heard Ronnie talking. The plan was to be utterly quiet once inside, which we now were, in order to not attract attention. Besides, who could he be talking too??!!

I stood up straight to see what could be going on over there just in time to see Ronnie running towards the house, halfway there he began to wave a greeting as though he saw someone he knew in the house. When he bounded upon the porch, clearly with glee, the front door opened allowing entrance. Without pause, Ronnie ran right into the house and the door closed sounding the finality of a prison gate; a life lost. The house had swallowed him.

I looked to the left, and Bruce too had observed this astounding behavior, and was clearly as astonished as I was. What could possibly possess someone, knowing what we all know about this place, to behave in this manner?

My bones told me there was no chance of going into that house. I looked at Bruce, blankly; implying that the decision was his and all the while hoping that he too would decline to follow Ronnie.

His bones told him the opposite. We could not leave without Ronnie.

Damn!

Reluctantly, we approached each other at full height; the secret shroud of our arrival had evaporated. We were already announced, by Ronnie's unbelievable behavior. It never occurred to us that we were in fact being invited in. That is why the mesmerizing effect that had sent everyone else home, did not impact us. Without speaking, we agreed to rescue our friend. Shoulder to shoulder, we turned to look at the Grey House where we would face whatever fate awaits.

But wait! Not the front door. Let's take a walk around the house, there is probably some broken screen door to the kitchen, or rotted out gateway to the basement, or something. Here is where our skills at sneaking into all those football stadiums and carnivals come in handy; we will find a way in; but it will be *our* way in, not the front door.

The very back of the house did have what used to be a screen-enclosed porch off the kitchen. Carefully, cause we could ill afford to have ourselves injured by rotten porch timber, we approached the kitchen door. The screen on the door had completely rotted away also. All I had to do was push my hand through the remaining screen, which instantly turned to dust, and unhook the simple lock.

We were in the kitchen.

To our utter amazement, the kitchen had towering cabinets scaling two of the walls. There was a table in the middle that was tall enough for us to walk under without bending our heads at all.

On the table there were apples the size of basketballs. Closer inspection, however, revealed that they were actually grapes. It finally dawned on us that whoever inhabited this place had to in fact be of monstrous proportions. With considerable effort, we returned our attention to the urgent task of finding Ronnie and getting out.

Since he came in the front door, let's start there.

Silently, we found our way towards the front of the house. We passed what appeared to be a reading room, equipped just like the kitchen, with a table taller than us, and bookcases populated with strangely labeled, old, hard covered texts, that would have been too large for us to even retrieve from the shelves. We continued towards what had to be the front of the house where Ronnie, stupid Ronnie, just had to come inside!

Impossibly, the inside of this 'house' was of colossal proportions totally belied by the outward appearance.

The inside was just like the outside; never attended to. We were able to see Ronnie's footprints as they came in the front door in the thick dust that covered the floor. They went to the (his) left upon entering, the opposite direction from which we had just come.

As we proceeded in this direction, to the right was a lofty, curved staircase, with enormity more than human, that went up to a second floor which surrounded the entire house it seemed with a walkway with many doors and several halls that wound off into utter and hollow darkness. Cautiously, we followed the footprints; thankful they did not lead upstairs. We need to find him fast before fear overtakes us and changes our minds completely.

Very faintly, I could hear a strangely familiar muffled sound coming from the direction we were going. We moved over to the wall, so that we could inch our way forward and defeat the chances of being discovered by...anything that may be in this place.

Fortunately, very shortly the familiar sounds were recognized as those made by a considerably large number of people dining together.

We squeezed ourselves along the wall until we came upon a large room before us, where, there was in fact a large table with what appeared to be about 20 people sitting around it eating.

Crouching behind a small table that was holding a dim lamp, we could make out the entire group across the hallway without being noticed. It took a few moments, but; I did recognize Billy Mitchell sitting at the table.

Billy was a classmate of mine, two years earlier. More than a classmate, we were actually quite good friends. Billy and his family had moved to Detroit; yet, those were his parents on either side of him, eating in relative silence.

There was also Trudy Jones. I would never forget her because, even though she was several years older, I had a boyhood crush on her for as long as I could remember. But, she was no longer older than me. In fact, she was exactly the same age as the last summer before she left this town.

There were several other people recognizable at the table. But in every case, it was someone, or some family, who had 'moved away', or otherwise relocated, to some other distant place. But they were in fact all right here! They had not gone anywhere! And they looked exactly as they had when they 'left'. Trudy was no longer older than me. Not *this* Trudy.

Then we saw Billy's dog Apache. The dog had died a year before Billy and his family moved to Detroit. It was sitting by Billy's leg at the table. A position I clearly recall that his parents would not allow at dinner because I often visited them in those days.

We made no noise at all. Suddenly, as if by clairvoyance; the dog immediately swung his head around to look directly at us; he looked as though my very recognition of him had made a suspicious sound that he could hear. His ears twitched, and he instantly sprang to his feet, and began to snarl like Cerberus, guarding the gates of Hades. This was effectively an alarm to everyone at the table who also immediately ceased all activity and, without searching, turned their laser like attention upon us.

I could feel the heat from their glare; eyes rimmed with deep bloody red. Inhuman forked tongues darted out of several mouths in serpent like fashion. They rose from the table in unison; never taking their eyes off us…

Without a word, we turned and ran. We ran back across the large foyer that comprised the entryway. Looking over my shoulder to see the 'missing people' storming out of the dining room after us, only, they were running on all fours; backs arching like true quadrupeds in pursuit. Now their tongues wagged out of their open mouths like wolves. And they howled like a pack of wild animals.

Their form of locomotion, along with the changes in their bodies, made it clear they were soon going to overtake us. In utter desperation we decided to run, jump, up the staircase; because we all know, canines are not so graceful on stairs as they are on open ground.

To our surprise, they did not even pursue us up the stairs. They came to a screeching halt, some tumbling in the dust under their own momentum. Reverting to human, upright posture, they walked back and forth at the bottom of the stairs staring with those empty red rimmed eyes, long tongues rolling out of their mouths like a dog on a hot day. Some of them had long snake like tails trailing behind them.

We stumbled up the stairs backwards. Looking at them, in case they changed their minds…

We reached the second story of the house. From here, looking upwards, the very top of the building hosted a huge glass dome. Through it I could see the most magnificent display of brilliant stars and other features never seen before – clouds of erupting gas, against a palpably thick, blue-black sky. I knew I was somehow closer to the entire Universe than I had ever been before. This was not a scene one could commonly see from the surface of the earth. Besides, it was full daylight still when we entered the house.

I looked back down the stairs and they were all gone. Nowhere to be seen. Since Ronnie was not among them, we decided to see if he was upstairs also. Maybe he was fortunate enough to have escaped them in the same way we just did. Either way, without discussion: getting out of here is already far more important than finding Ronnie (stupid Ronnie).

With all the noise echoing throughout the mansion from the chase just escaped, there is no need to try to be quiet. Anything that can hear already knows we are here by now.

There was a huge, ominous door at the end of the hallway before us.

When the door opened, the wind of death floated out onto the balcony. Standing in the doorway was a very tall (far more than human height), large, muscular figure, of a man. Those tables and books belonged to him. He did not move, but his very presence exuded sheer gravity. This was an entity that encompassed more than mortals have ever witnessed before.

It was as if some two story tall, granite statue in the main lobby of a bustling New York skyscraper had awakened; infuriated by the way that mankind had exploited his true immortal grandeur to adorn their meager buildings. This was the infernal rage before us now.

With the sound of thunder, heard on the inside; in the space of an instant, eons were revealed to us, as if flying through the galaxy. His intent was not instruction, or sharing; we could see these phenomena simply as a by-product of having been brought into his mind. His intent was examination of us.

One could feel that what he was doing with the missing people was consuming their future, extracting all the promise from their lives; their hopes and dreams; this is what he lived on. Simple manipulation, crushing several dreams, diminishing just a little celestial light, is how he victimized them; exactly as a spiders poison incapacitates the victim. It was a combination of this and the wind from his home world blowing in this place that transformed them into the creatures they were becoming; Man is never far from Monster – human aspiration is a feeble barrier.

I grabbed Bruce's arm, to set him into motion as I turned to flee. The grab meant I was not going to wait – better come now! With my acceleration being so desperate, the ancient carpet beneath my feet rolled, fighting my intention to escape and catapulting my mind into complete terror. But I kept running. Bruce was energized into action by my grasp of his arm, and he too managed to turn and flee.

The creature in the doorway, actually filling the huge doorway, did not bother to pursue us. Pursuit never entered his vast mind. You do not chase mosquitoes; you kill them when they light on your arm again.

We ran back past the stairs. Looking down, those people were once again, all gathered around the bottom of the staircase. That path was blocked. We kept running until we came upon a very narrow stairway at the opposite side of the second level. At a glance, the stairs were more normal size, and this stairway did not even open up on the level where the 'people' were because we did not see it when we were downstairs. It actually was a servants egress. Apparently for human sized servants.

The stairway was interminably long as it had no exit on the first floor but continued uninterrupted into the cellar. This did not feel good at all. With what we have seen already, is not the cellar in this place bound to be far worse?

No stopping now. At this point we have to concentrate on saving ourselves.

Upon arriving at the bottom, one entire wall, of what appeared to be a recently excavated basement, the length of a football field was lined with embedded cages lit with mildly different colored lights from the top of each cell. Some were filled with a writhing mist that did not escape what appeared to be a set of horizontal and vertical bars encasing each cage. This was a menagerie that provided the many beasts within, a recreation of the environment from whatever world he was taken from.

Just then, a beast resembling a huge grizzly bear covered with alligator skin crashed into the bars of his cage with such ferocity that it physically shook many of the adjacent cages and elicited a huge cacophony of growls and shrieks from the nearby inhabitants.

My extreme terror was revealed with an audible shriek of my own.

Then, I felt myself gripped from behind on the shoulder. My entire life dissolved inside me as I turned around to find that it was Ronnie, standing behind us.

Ronnie was trying to explain to us what had occurred. He spoke slowly, actually he mumbled. I could see his cheek quickly jutting out, as though his tongue were poking it. It fell upon me in a flash; Ronnie too has the serpent tongue, and he was trying to hide it from us!

Just like the dog before him, 'Ronnie' knew instantly he had been discovered. He pounced upon me, with more power than he had ever possessed, forcing me backwards against one of the cages of the enclosed beasts. Behind me I could actually feel the delight (the hunger) of the creature within as it began to slither towards the bars of the cage and receive this human offering which was myself.

In spite of our history of my superior athletic prowess, I could not even begin to contest Ronnie's strength at this point. Bruce too, attempted in vain to force Ronnie to relinquish his grasp upon me. With utter ease, he ignored Bruce, and he pinned me against the bars as the creature within increased his speedy approach, beckoning my certain doom.

It is said that man's extremity is Gods opportunity. There was certainly only one single moment left for me; and looking deep within Ronnie's eyes I was surprised to see recognition. In that instant, our entire shared childhood passed between us, both good and bad, and with the same complete power that he had pinned me against the bars, he now jerked me away. Behind me, I could hear the creature within crashing, disappointed, against the cage, furious at the lost opportunity.

Speechless, and with an inhuman, mechanical like precision, Ronnie pointed towards a sizable nook within the cavernous walls of this dungeon. As we peered within the nook, we could see a stairway with light squeezing through the edges at the top. We turned to thank him only to see him turn and run with supernatural speed down the length of the walkway between the cages, uttering guttural, primordial grunts along the way, until something from within one of the cages reached out and pulled him in. His sounds ended abruptly, signaling certain extermination.

We chose to ascend the stairs.

There was the outside, old fashion cellar door at the top, which was not even locked. We opened it with ease to emerge into the same un-kept yard we had just left. As we shut the cellar doors we could still hear the cries from the unholy collection of wildlife below. The only difference being that it had to be about midnight judging from the position of the moon, the darkness, and the quiet that seemed to surround the neighborhood as far as we could tell.

Why did Ronnie not secure my death? Perhaps he was in the initial stages of being 'absorbed' by this place. More likely, the colossal creature within – who clearly spanned eons and galaxies – perhaps he had no concept of simple human friendship: A situation he had not incurred as yet. For whatever reason, at whatever stage of being 'taken over' he was at, the 'Ronnie' on the inside was being made from the Ronnie we knew. I do not think the being upstairs could just invent heroism, or even recognize it. Even if he could, he would not employ it to act for our sake. No, this incubus, this voodoo doll that was to become Ronnie, somehow was being made from the real thing – our friend.

Amazingly, when we finally got back outside, there was Ronnie, excited, asking us why we just suddenly ran into the house – for no reason! This inquiry was so honestly set forth as to disarm us of any anger or other misgivings at all. This was our Ronnie. I could see the tinge of guilt in his eye for not coming after us – he had no hint that we had encountered 'him' on the inside of this place. I could also appreciate his dilemma; and at least he did not leave the yard. He was just unable to get into the house. He did not realize that the 'Ronnie' that was on the inside, was a part of him, and this meant too that a part of him was a true hero, in a way that this, our Ronnie, would perhaps never know.

And, it was the right decision in the end…the creature within had easily fooled us all.

And there was no old woman at all, contrary to a popular rumor.

And, *most* importantly, Ronnie had recovered the ball.

Little Lies

By Kenneth G. Gary

Prelude

And what of the silent crimes, the ones that no one else perceives? Does it not exist except in the sight of the un-confessed perpetrator? Or does it have a life of its very own, born of a stolen part of the heart of he who authors the untruth. There is no solace, no escape; offenses adhere to the soul, and the eternal engraving is etched ever deeper...

- The wretched

Once Upon A Time...

Makela and Fenu felt like it was their special place. Siblings have that extra measure of unspoken understanding, that special way of seeing things that only they can see. This special place was a far corner of the barn where the livestock was kept. It was always warm there because there were no windows on that end of the barn.

Makela was 10 and Fenu, her younger brother, as far as she knew, was 7 or 8. They were adopted from an orphanage, and they did not possess definitive records.

Makela was rather mischievous. She enjoyed slipping several tiny, and actually harmless, pebbles into the pig's trough so she could hear them squeal in pain when their teeth crashed against the surprises hidden within their food.

Makela was the very *picture of pretty* with her long brown braids down her back, wearing old, worn blue overalls and a thin feminine flowered blouse.

Fenu was very adept at the tricks he could play. It was a skill perfected at the large orphanage they had come from, where there were many children and little supervision. He was small for his age, he also had curly, bushy hair that appeared to be multi colored in the summer sun. Not realizing how wonderful it really was, in a fall foliage kind of way, he was gravely insulted any time anyone mentioned it.

Some of Fenu's expertise was necessary survival skills in a tumultuous environment; but some of it was an expression of unbridled anger, and worse, an enjoyment in the suffering of others.

While not federal crimes, still, they were always sinister, and, so cleverly devised that Fenu would nearly always escape all blame. Children devise ways of surviving at an orphanage that is unlike those methods found otherwise in homes and schools.

This farm, which had become their new home, had an old house needing another coat of white paint; but it was sturdy and large enough. It was a two-story building, a nice large porch with an unfinished attic used for storage. The front yard had two gigantic trees on either side of the walkway that provided gracious quantities of shade. The large barn sorely needed repair. It appeared to never have been painted and was structurally not more than a big box.

The work that they did on this farm was very demanding.

There was the seemingly endless collection of crops, herding and feeding of animals, cooking of meals and cleaning afterwards; all of which was followed by severe homework that would secure several strikes from a ruler if not completed.

Worst of all, mostly because there is always some arbitrary complaint that takes center stage in ones day, they deplored bringing in the chickens at night. This had to be done to prevent some Chicken Hawks from swooping down and decimating the flock. Or, a Coyote, who could squeeze under the fence and kill a dozen chickens. Or, maybe chickens just die because it is dark and they are afraid; they die of fear; either way, they were an investment and they had to be protected.

They did not like this place where they had to work endlessly.

Being of severely modest means, often, the only escape into childhood joy that they knew was running thru the woods. The great, comforting woods. One afternoon while they were feeding the pigs…

Makela whispered, "C'mon Fenu, they are not looking." She was referring to the farmer and his wife

Fenu, worried, "We do not need to get into trouble."

Makela, "They will just think we are in the barn. C'mon."

Makela grabbed Fenu's arm and pulled him the first few steps and they were off running towards the woods.

The trees were very tall, with dark bark. Makela liked the way their shadows stretched along the ground like artwork.

Although no one was vocal about it, these woods were permeated with a great aura due to their proximity to a great source…a source these kids were soon to discover.

There was a deep lake in the middle of these woods. A strange lake; for, the people of the town had observed that even when the wind blew with ferocious strength, this lake never yielded the slightest ripple upon its surface.

This was no ordinary lake. The lake did provide fish, on every single attempt, and it maintained a smile like quality upon the lives of the people in the Village. There was one exception: there was always a dense mist in the middle, stretching from one side to the other. It was a natural barrier, keeping them on this side of the lake. No one had ever gone into this mist and returned.

One evening, when the mountain of work was nearing completion, all the chickens they had painfully gathered got out. They ran, jumped and half flew, as chickens will do, to all ends of the farm. Some even left and went as far as a nearby creek and drowned. Some ended up getting caught in barbed wire fences – and died, and some were never found again at all.

Everyone was chasing them. The farmer, his wife and the kids. The former were experienced at handling the birds; not Makela and Fenu.

Every chicken they did catch pecked and scratched at them, drawing blood on occasion. These injuries morphed into insult by the fact that they were saving these ignorant creatures that had the temerity to injure them in their effort to do so. Makela kicked one or two of them when no one could see her.

Makela, whispering to Fenu "We should let these things go. Who cares what happens to them".

Fenu "They're biting me hard! I don't want to catch these chickens!"

Farmer, overhearing him, "Grab the bird by the neck from behind, boy. See how I do it? Now keep fetching those birds!"

Makala and Fenu were punished for this unfortunate event – they had left a gate open. For weeks they went without privileges, and were given extra work. The children tried desperately to address this increase in their tasks, only to find themselves increasingly frustrated.

Over time, the children felt a silent objection to all their work mounting to near explosion within them.

Eventually, since they were orphans anyway, they decided to escape from this place. They decided to get into the rowboat that was always on the shore of the Great Lake and go to the other side. They had been on their own before and were not afraid of facing it again.

They got in the boat, and rowed until they could no longer move their arms. It was already late and, in spite of the stories they had heard, they decided to go straight through the mist that inhabited the center of the lake.

The Mist put them to sleep.

When they arrived on the other side, they felt not only warm air, but air that was almost full of caressing hands. One could not see the source of this subtle and divine grooming – the way a mother shuffles her hands thru the hair of a child, a completely casual, unexplained and unique affection, for seemingly no reason at all. It is just the way this world is.

There was a group awaiting them on the shore. They appeared to be relatively small, but healthy people and there was the distinct sense that their arrival was somehow expected. Standing several steps in front of the group was someone who clearly had a special interest in their arrival. He stood nearest to the shore leading the welcoming committee. He, too, had unruly, multi colored locks very much like Fenu.

As time progressed, they would find that their new friend is best described as youthful but wise, thin but possessed with great agility. The unbelievable light in his eye, (all eyes shine with the brightness, and hue, of the soul within) was only innocence: it was not the character of brightness thru bleariness that announces a soul, which has won peace thru severe battle. He, was clearly a child of the bright blue sky. And he looked vaguely familiar too.

"Greetings. My name is Mishma" he announced, extending his hand to assist Makela from the boat.

They were led to a small village. As they visited dwellings, which could not be properly called houses, because these people lived nearly outside in the world. While there were some permanent structures for meetings and such, they erected no walls that would only block the sweet wind and familiar breeze that seemed to constantly move – as regular as the breath of an entire planet. What a wondrous place.

There was no work to speak of (no comparison to the place they had just left); what work there was, was so joyously enjoined that one hardly could call it work. However, the results were never what was intended and did little to help sustain their lives. In fact, Makela wondered, *if there is a winter in this place, these people are going to starve*! They seemed to only gather enough for the day at hand.

One day, Mishma took them on a long walk thru a most glorious meadow, there was heard a low, rumbling sound. It felt as though the distant mountains were beginning to walk. It resounded thru heaven and earth, it was felt on the inside too, *where thoughts are born*.

This was the most unsettling feeling ever...Makela never knew that something could possibly reach through her heart and into her soul so deeply, so easily, and so completely. What Makala did not know was that the buffers that exist between Man and the Universe in her world, which allows a falsified existence, were simply absent in this one.

The casual reporting of this event to the tribal council that evening brought the first colors of consternation to the eyes of their hosts. In fact, one could see a *history* of terror in their eyes now. A flood of fear swept over Makala and Fenu. But the council only listened, glancing at one another: they did not comment.

While Makela did not find their restraint even remotely comforting, it did deflate her desire to relay what she thought to be a sign of some kind at least. But, maybe it was just distant thunder after all, in spite of how it actually felt. *And once again, as happens so often in life, the subjugation of what one suspects to be vital information occurred...* she finally let it go.

The orchards were out in the open, adjacent to the vast plains. Then there was brush and rocks before reaching the more dense forest which increased in density as one progressed. Deep in this safe forest is where they lived.

On a later evening, while completing a long, but enjoyable afternoon of collecting fruits,

Fenu, "Hey 'Kayla, want a plum?"

Makayla, holding out her palm, "Sure. Why is it squishy on one side?"

Fenu, wiping his palms on his pants, "Just came that way, I guess."

When she was half through eating, Fenu whirled around and throw a strike hitting Mishma in the back of his head with another 'plum'.

Mishma, jerking his head around "Hey, who..."

Fenu "She did it! Look at the purple juice running down her wrist."

Mishma "Why you..."

Mishma began playfully chasing them through the orchard.

The noise erupted again. This time it was clearly malevolently surrounding them with its evil. Soon, on the horizon, the very incarnation of this sound of fury, like a pot that has begun to boil rapidly, began to gallop across the plains to meet them. They could tell that whatever was coming had honed into their hearts, and was targeting them in a radar like fashion – so much so that there was a virtual heat like phenomenon haunting them as they, and their host, instinctively sought coverage.

What was first a distant cloud of dust became a rumbling collection of beasts: Terrible, boiling, titanic beasts. It could now be seen that their speed was achieved by 'riding' upon the backs of a variety of equally hideous quadrupeds; animals that seemed consigned as well as their masters, to the entire hell inspired ordeal. The terror that they would traverse the plains with the speed of bison immediately gripped Fenu and Makala's hearts with the certainty of no escape.

Mishma ushered them through the thick underbrush into the woods. Everyone else who was in the orchards was racing towards the woods also. There were terrible screams of some who were too far out on the fringe of the orchard to escape. As the beasts arrived at the orchard, those straddling other beasts dismounted. They were too large to progress much further while mounted. The pursuit continued on foot, at a much slower pace.

The kids could hear the shrieks of some who did not make good in their escape attempt.

Their eyes were the most noticeable. They were searching eyes, the kind that police appear to have when *you* have committed a crime; a feeling born of your own guilt – they knew your secrets! They were glowing eyes, the kind that reveal a barely contained, even greater monster on the *inside.*

These ravenous monsters, armed with saber teeth and claws, had a caustic odor that forced the perfume like atmosphere to shrink away, the flowers and trees shriveled upon attack from the growing putrescence. The growing herd of terrific monsters surged forward, towards them at the end of the plain in the scant coverage of trees where they had hoped to survive.

There was no mistaking the savage countenance of these beasts, and their eyes were now the source of extreme terror. Worst of all, by far, they were *familiar* eyes, the kind that one has seen before. In the meeting of Man and Monster, this was more than the common revulsion of physically hideous features; although these marauding creatures were hideous enough; there was that feint grin on the Monsters face, the obvious pleasure he would take in destroying you, but the even greater pleasure in making you quake with fear: making a tear in your soul, leaving you to a fate not known to man or beast before.

They ran, they hid, they had a guide who was extremely quick and wise about the woods; Mishma. He knew before the sound that the beasts had arrived, He knew their behavior like the animals they were. But in spite of being such, they had a special ability to appeal, with all their gory detail - To the hearts of some men: they just seemed to *know* you.

Their escape was narrow. Racing back to camp Mishma led them through the thickest of the woods with impenetrable underbrush. The children, and Mishma could squeeze through, but the rampaging monsters could not, not at their gigantic size.

That evening, upon mentioning that he, Fenu, had recognized the beast as familiar, his observation gave immediate pause; and unbridled terror, to all who could hear it. He was immediately marshaled off into the place the council met; a larger thatched structure, with only his sister, Mishma, and one of the elders.

It was Makela who then began to recall what affected her the most about one of the beasts that had come charging through the bushes in her direction – ripping hedges from the very ground and tearing, no, searing, the bark from trees with the acid on his skin.

She told of how there was a strange slowness to the entire scene. She told of how her escape was thwarted by an unexpected slowness in her body upon attempting to run – like she was running through some thick and viscous liquid: or as if her body was strangely anesthetized and there was very little muscular response to what was an absolutely horrific moment. Almost as if something within her *wanted* to get caught.

Their hosts listened without speaking....

She went on to describe how haunting the eyes were. How they looked at her 'sideways', as if to insure that she witnessed these events;, and how the monster seemed to enjoy heightening her suffering by pretending to chase someone else for a moment - long enough for her to feel a slight hope of escape (even at the expense of some of the others: genuine horror makes cowards or heroes of us all) – only to swing around instantly in an even more vigorous and menacing pursuit of her.

Fenu's silence went unnoticed. He had felt, deeply, how these beasts had instant and intimate contact with the raging feelings that he directed at others at the orphanage. All the things he had escaped from before, all his mean tricks, which he thought he had escaped punishment from, were burning in the eyes and 'side way glances' of these spirit quaking beasts.

Fenu's concerns were noticed by one - by Mishma, whose hair virtually sparkled in the exact multicolored way that Fenu's did at the moment.

With that said, all the members of the smaller council became animated in a way that was clearly not usual for them. They all began to speak in turn…

"They must be told! Or we shall perish!" exclaimed one of the council.

"They cannot be *told:* they must discover"

"They do not see it! They never see it!"

"Your kind has been here before. They walk our world and constantly exclaim what a miracle it is. Will they never see that they are the miracle? The ugly, deep and fleeting joy at the ill fate of another, even a friend, these seemingly private and hidden enjoyments of what you know to be wrong…"

"– don't you see that *thoughts are things*!! At least, yours are for us. Everything about you is miraculous, you can learn to read and write, you can learn to excel at anything!

Your thoughts create the weather in our world! They can be Sunny or Stormy. It matters!!

"The Man on death row does not contribute to the hordes of beasts that plague our world – he is meeting his fate and judgment in your world. It is the seemingly minor, *unpaid* crimes that find their way into our world and cause untold suffering. We pay for your *little lies* and broken promises"

"It was YOU that gave birth to the beast! That is the reason for the familiar look in his eye, to you. You know that he recognized you! – he belongs to you!. You broke a promise, you uttered a falsehood, you may have forsaken a friend. We know not what it was, but your minor crimes, the ones that you never get caught in and never pay a price for, are the seeds that create these vast herds of murderous beasts that tear through our awnings at night and eat our children alive in their beds."

"What can we do to fix things?!" Makela cried.

"The only way you can help us is to go back to your world: the only world we know of *where you can make the sun shine as bright as you wish*. Go back and fulfill your promises, go back and bear your burdens with silent dignity – only fight battles that are *worthy*, not frivolous, go back and cleanse your heart that our children may survive!"

"Can you tell me exactly how to behave when I return, to put an end to this suffering?"

The three elders seated in a semi circle around the fire each spoke in turn;

"If that were possible, it would have been done long ago, don't you think? We would gladly have written a book of rules that would save our lives should you adhere to it. Dogma never suffices. And, if we were able to do that, there would no longer be a reason for you or for us to exist."

"If you knew for sure there was a god, in the way you know there is a fire before you now, there would be no need for faith or a quest for truth – you could just saunter down to 25 Heavenly Lane and all things would already be answered. That would take more meaning out of your life than you could imagine."

"The number that you win must be greater than the number that you lose. But, no one knows what this number is...so you must live in complete awareness of this balance, and try as hard as you can to keep the positive above the negative, because you do not know where the line is. What other strategy is there but to constantly try as hard as you can?"

Makela stood up and asked:

"One last question. Where do you people really come from and why do you know so much about this relationship with our world? You said it 'may be our last chance', as if there is possibly more than one. How did you know?"

By now, everyone else was entering the scantily built building, drawn by the voices.

It was their guide, Mishma that answered:

"I was Human once. I could not see the divine gift of sheer potential. I was blinded by pursuit of goals that were not worthy of the greatness of Man, but merely catered to my own selfish, pointless, desires..."

Just then, the door burst open so violently that dust and debris instantly exuded from every crevice in the entire abode. In the doorway stood a huge Wolf like creature that appeared to have been perhaps a man once. He gave a mighty roar of triumph and rushed forward grabbing the people, two or three in each hand. Everyone screamed and scrambled to and fro seeking escape but this huge predator was a ravenous Shark amongst a school of small fish.

The screams were soul rending.

With the door open, other, even more terrifying beasts poured into the room…

These huge monsters waded through the opening one after another, each one more terrible than the one before. They grabbed the scattering woods people in iron claws by the handful; and stuffed them into their gaping mouths. One could hear a tempest of growls and cries, of predation and death. These monsters were driven by inexorable powers, and the people were consumed in an ever-recurring drama.

As selfish as it may seem, the children, Makala and Fenu could do nothing about this invasion. They did the only thing they could do: Makala took Fenu's hand firmly, and began to run. Amazingly, they were able to make their way towards the door successfully. Finally, after dodging through the legs of a towering monster, they got to the door and out. They ran breathlessly towards the lake – for they could hear the crashing of trees behind them, and it was getting closer.

There was a short time where, Makela held her brother in her right hand, on her left side Mishma was running right beside her too. One glance at his face revealed that not only his unusual hair, but also his entire expression was an exact replica of Fenu's. Makela did not allow another question to enter her mind. Instantly, she shoved Mishma from the path and doubled her effort to sprint to shore with her brother still in the tight grip of her right hand.

They will never forget the shattering mortal sounds of terror they could hear calling behind them.

Once they got to the boat and began to row back to their side… somehow, they knew the water offered safety - she could see Mishma standing on the shore, unable to catch the boat, an exact replica of Fenu, and dejected. This was not the ending he had in mind. Makala was remorseful as well; what if Mishma, knowing what he knows, could actually make both worlds better?

But it did not matter. Fenu is her brother.

Fenu: "What do you think he meant when he said 'you can make the sun shine as bright as you wish'"?

Makala: "I think he meant that we can be as happy as we want to be, or as good at something as we want to be. Maybe he meant that we have no limits at all. I don't know."

"I also think that Mishma meant to take your place on our side of the lake."

As their boat progressed across the Mist one could hear…the sound of a woeful wind, the kind that portends a storm, or, a change of life. Hearing this ominous sound, but wishing to comfort her brother, Makela said:

"C'mon. Let's go see if the chickens need to be put back inside for the night."

The Treasure

By Kenneth G. Gary

Prelude

"There are more things in heaven and earth, Horatio, than are dreamt of in your philosophy."

- Hamlet, William Shakespeare

Once upon a Time.........
Back when the world was being formed, back when monsters and demons themselves were windswept entities, they too had to wait. They had to wait until man himself evolved to register as a form of sustenance for them. Until then, they hungered, and raged as they longed for nourishment...

There was a small village, in the 'old country', where peasants knew little but knew what was important, or, all that was derived of fear: they knew not to be caught on the roadside at night during the full moon, they knew not to be rummaging thru the root cellar after dark. They knew not to tempt creatures that fly at night, and scream throughout the heavens. They knew that terror and horror colored the distant walls of their world.

Some could not be so convinced, however. There was a child, a boy who had an insatiable propensity for inquisition. To the towns people he was merely rambunctious: stealing pies set upon window sills to cool, crawling beneath the sacred chambers of the church, throwing rocks into the ever still pond. As legend has it, the pond harbored the most hideous beasts known to man, long ago captured by heroes long dead, which strained and called out to man in his dreams in a constant effort to gain their terrible freedom. Freedom to stalk the earth, yea, the very soul of man, to render every household, church and meeting place unto a place susceptible to the demons that wish to tear their way into this world.

But it is the Soul of Man that is the doorway. Who watches this opening; who protects against the ever-present dangers that seek entrance…

One day, the boy, Thorneous, was particularly inspired to commit mischief. He did not know why, but there was a special energy in his step that sought to also do something that he had not done before, something novel. He was bored.

He was an avid listener of the stories the elders would tell around the fireplace. In spite of his mischievous nature, they really adored him and were even inspired by his attention to their stories.

On this day, the boy remembered hearing a story about treasures being hidden deep within the Great Woods. These are the woods where his people never cut the trees to be used for building their houses, where hunters never set traps or ventured in pursuit of game; no one ever dared enter unless they were ready to lose their very life.

He went there anyway…

At the edge of the Great Woods, even Thorneous was stopped dead in his tracks by the strange character of the low winds that blew thru these woods. It was thicker, even wetter than normal wind. No, it actually seemed to carry ill intent, as though it had just passed some scene of indescribable terror.

He entered anyway…

Thorneous was driven part by adventure, part by challenge, part by a dim desire to actually find the treasures he had heard of in the elders stories: But mostly, he was simply compelled, and he did not even know why.

He went further into the Great Woods...

It was not very long before Thorneous found an ancient tree. This tree was so large around that it took 100 paces to circle round it – just like the tales the elders told.

"This must be the place!" screamed his heart with joy! Not out loud, for he was adventurous but not foolish.

Thorneous circled the august structure (for in spite of his audacity, he was not without respect in the end) until he finally noticed that beneath one of the huge roots protruding from the trunk, there was what appeared to be a dark…opening, just spacious enough to allow him to squeeze himself inside.

Thorneous slowly descended what may have once actually been a paved stairway, but was now covered with a collection of large writhing roots that fortunately allowed access to a large opening at the bottom. He found himself within a large chamber, he thought, because no light from above was permitted penetration to this depth. But, like any animal, he had a feeling for the size of the area he was in.

Thorneous instantly began to investigate his surroundings. He had several wooden matches with him. Carefully, he lit one match and tried to hold it up above his head to gain vision of his entire surroundings. No sooner had he lifted the match up than it was extinguished, as if by invisible breath.

"Who's there??!!!" he gasped, surprised at the tremulous sound of his own voice.

No answer. He lit another only to find the same occurrence. This went on until his matches were nearly gone. The next match, for he had in his rising panic staggered near what was one of the walls of the chamber, this next match found a lantern of some sort directly above its flame, which promptly caught fire casting light throughout the cavern. He could have sworn that just beyond the edge of his peripheral vision he detected the wraith like nature of something that scampered to avoid contact with the poisonous light from the lamp.

With amazing relief, and unbelievable bravery, Thorneous began to search for treasure. He was anxious to depart these premises as he felt the entire place was aware of his presence.

The ceiling was surprisingly high and gently curved towards the walls. The walls themselves and floor were merely dug out of the ground. They appeared to have been packed so hard it made them quite sturdy. There were several chambers visible, and a corridor he hoped he would not have to investigate.

There were objects; dry, dusty, odd-looking things that were placed against walls and on several small tables almost as if they were macabre decorations where most would have placed lamps and flowers. Terribly, some of them seemed to be human skulls, and entire human bodies that had been sufficiently shrunk to be contained within small wire cages.

In the middle of the cavern there were rows of very large chairs spaciously placed with precision in a semi circle, with a raised structure resembling a judge's desk at the open end; and, an aisle that passed in the middle of what could be a seated audience.

Needless to say, his fear rapidly mounted. Thorneous searched desperately for treasure of some sort when he painfully stubbed his toe on a large wooden chest against the far wall that he did not even see. Without hesitation he opened it …on the way up his mind said "what if this is a casket and there is a salivating Vampire within….." but it was too late. Besides, there were only stunning, brightly glittering treasures within!

Thorneous did not even realize that his entire being was arrested for a moment in sheer, overwhelming joy at his discovery! Sometimes the mind can see everything in a moment: he could see large crowns that must have been worn by Kings, he could see necklaces that would elicit jealousy from Nefertiti, these gold's and riches were so great that they sang out to him – He could hear the metallic ring from the jewels – like an Angelic choir…and then, he heard the grumbling, terrible noises from above.

Something else was entering the tree under the root just as he had done. He could tell from the nonchalant character of the low grumbling and growling that he was soon to be joined by something of horrible demeanor that was entering this place not for the first time; It was his home. In fact, there was more than just one; it sounded like a group of inebriated sailors returning to their ship. He ran across the room, blew out the lamp on the wall, ran back across to the chest, jumped in and quietly closed the lid.

Thorneous was exploding with terror as he heard what turned out to be a vast procession of......creatures, descending into the chamber with growls and roars that clearly indicated they were attacking one another on the way down the stairs, the way that lions in the circus may do in passing at times.

Soon, he could see light. There was a small enough knothole in the wood of the chest where he was hidden that if he turned slowly enough, and quietly enough, he could see into the room. And this is what he witnessed...

The Meeting is Called to Order

He listened as someone, *something*, insisted that a hush should pervade the room, such that an orderly encounter might ensue; for there was a large collection of *dark creatures* seated by this time.

The Monsters took the stage first. A large, gray, uneven shaped creature began to walk to the center of the room. The gray aspect of his nature was most marked. With one huge hairy shoulder noticeably higher than the other, throwing his head off to an angle, and a gait that revealed uneven length to his thick legs and elephantine feet, he moved center stage with the expectation of delivering his special message.

As he approached, you could hear a grating and growling sound issuing forth. But this sound did not come from his throat. It came from his soul...you could feel it in your own. These Monsters are not separate from us at all.

First Monster

He sat in the chair in the middle of the chamber. His considerable girth made the ancient wooden chair cry out. Comfort was gained by leaning back, allowing his huge, hairy shoulders to be supported by the back of the chair, while extending his legs, which now ended in large prehensile, clawed feet. This was a frame that clothing simply could not encompass. He actually seemed to posses some innate potential that wished to escape his very body.

He began to speak of one of his most treasured haunts. It was a child. A child that had to sleep upstairs alone. A child that suffered silently, knowing that no one would believe that there really was a monster in his closet. Even the monster did not know which was worse; that the child was terrorized by the monster, or the fact that no one would believe him. This is a unique human pain he observed, the pain of solitude, without the comfort of any understanding at all.

This monster told of how cunningly from his closet hideaway he held his breath while the boy's mother was in the room. The flaw this monster had was like ringing bells in your soul; the boy's mother would have known instantly of his presence, had he not held his breath, and his mind, as still as a pond on a windless day. She did notice an old, tattered shirt on a hanger at the end of the closet. She could not even recall purchasing the item, but it simply did not keep her attention. It was his perennial disguise, and it worked once again.

Once she was gone he would perform his best acts of fright.

He spoke of how he would make the closet door creak, causing the boy to jolt upright in his bed. He would then wait until the boy's suspicion would wane, only to cause an even louder creak! Again the boy would spring in fear completely upright in his bed; heart pounding, sweating, and wishing he could scream out to someone who would believe him. Like any infectious organism, you don't kill your host: It's your sustenance.

And Thorneous wondered why this Monster noticed the boys despair at all.

First Demon

A creature on the Demon side gave loud roaring sounds to catch the attention of all.

"This is the most common of all Monster tricks. You hide, you scare, you focus on little ones that are defenseless! You Monsters are weak! Let me tell you about the waves of terror I have sent throughout masses of mankind........."

There was almost nothing recognizable about this Demon in corporeal form. In fact, the closer one observed, the more it seemed to change. There was a ghastly swirling smoke surrounding he who had now secured the floor.

This Demon proceeded to speak of a time in the beginning of the century; He attempted many times but failed to fasten to the soul of Joseph Stalin himself; dictator of Russia after the first revolution.

But, one day, Stalin was particularly upset, and attending a large public dinner.

Drifting around the Grand Palatial room where the dinner was held, nearly made the Demon seasick, for, Demons are profoundly affected, in a storm like fashion, by collective human emotions, until they manage to take root!

Struggling, mightily, like being cast adrift from the Titanic – the Demon finally found the entrance to Stalin he was in search of. It was behind him, he had gone right past it; for this entrance is of the Soul, and had nothing to do with where Stalin was seated in the room.

Once he gained entrance, the Demon experienced the exultation that is comparable to that of a surfer in the Pacific – catching the 'dream wave'. He had no problem letting it guide him deep within Stalin's Soul.

Once within, he began to speak in the low voice of suspicion: A common favorite amongst Demons - as it often leads one to turn against those that were previously close. Next, over time, he added fury and self-righteousness. The songs this Demon was singing in Stalin's soul did not even reach Opera like proportions before Stalin succumbed and began to terrorize and extinguish people that were actually dedicated to his own cause!

This Demon went further to create such catastrophes that he and his kind, have subsisted to the current time on the Dividends thus secured. Demons thrive on the degree of destruction that they can inflict. They really have no choice, as surely as the Leopard must kill the wild boar, these Demons do what they were created for.

Second Monster

The next orator for the Monsters was an ancient, commanding creature (make no mistake, Thorneous could see clearly now that these processions were like a trial, or something). While he appeared extraordinarily well attired, in an immaculate black tuxedo with patent leather shoes that nearly glittered, he strode effortlessly, and gracefully, to middle of the semi circle, with a confidence and in a manner that revealed to anyone able to sense it; the long, ugly history of monstrous deeds performed with no concern for consequences. His was a spirit abjectly abandoned by all that is even remotely holy.

"We Monsters have always struck abject fear into the human heart. I have personally been on missions where we, through sheer gristling, gritting of teeth, and our best trick - reflection of the abysmal depths of human despair - have caused infirmities from insanity to cardiac arrest since time immemorial!"

The entire Monster cadre felt emboldened by such stories from one so venerable, and one could hear the loud gnashing of fangs, blowing of fire and gleaming of those terrible eyes that find you only when you are alone.

The Monster proceeded to tell his tale of ingenious means of frightening people nearly to death. He was a singularly inventive and patient Monster. Even some of his own kind felt he was a bit haughty. He was capable of hiding his face in a bowl of cereal, and just when you were about to ingest a spoonful, he would open his eyes wide, staring up at you from within the bowl between the flakes. Thus usually causing anyone who was his prey at the time, to drop the spoon, the cereal, and loose all their customary manners and run shrieking from the kitchen. Leaving everyone else to wonder what on such a bright sunny morning could possibly have incited such terror!

There were ripples of deep snorting laughter through the room at the recitation of such adventures.

Second Demon

But the Demons were not to be so easily challenged. Their next *witness* was also a Demon who had a legacy of centuries. He refused to provide his original, given name, to maintain his hidden heritage. It was a matter of discretion, he always claimed! In truth, he was a very ancient Demon, and his name was one of the keys that could render him vulnerable, and compromise his monumental powers.

He chose to appear in close to his natural form for impact. His form was one that barely contained the visions of the tortuous souls that he carried with him over the ages. Their inaudible screams, the faces of their tortured souls swirling around him, were a devastating phenomenon to behold.

For the first time in his life Thorneous felt naked terror.

Although he was an immensely powerful Demon, he had a particular fascination for delicately manipulating small, loving circles, and witnessing their self-destruction. He found it immensely gratifying, and, in fact, fulfilling. He often likened it to setting up elaborate structures of thousands of dominoes, which, when initiated, would fatefully collapse along preordained paths; all of which would be echoed by a parallel human tragedy. He felt himself the consummate conductor.

He did not detail any particular incident, but he literally swelled with pride when he revealed that it was He who, in visitations with William Shakespeare, inspired the character of Iago in the immortal story of Othello. The Demons were the learned population, and many of the Monsters were left wondering about the point in this instance.

Testimony after testimony revealed that the Demons claim that they are the more influential in that they do not chase humans down dark corridors, or crawl, unceremoniously, from beneath beds at night. Rather, they have the unique, the Divine right, to enter the soul of a human at the level where they can, if the human allows – *but no humans know this* – take control of the wheel of their life, their heart, their soul!

The Demons posit that this is a far superior role to play in the overall Celestial drama by taking control of the Human behavior, which begins by long, secretive manipulation of the emotions – hate, loathing, greed, envy, sloth, lack of self control - they are able to create Demonic Humans, in their behavior, which in some cases rival the extremes of essence such that it becomes impossible to distinguish between man and monster.

If no one else heard the real import of this message; Thorneous did.

Deliberation

The Monsters gathered themselves with increased confidence, and animosity. Their claim to influence is so vast, so overwhelming, that they have become common references: like, the monster under the bed, the monster in the closet, those 'things' that float thru the sky, just over your head as you proceed on your way home on a dark and rainy night.

The Demons, however, retorted once again, with the assertion that their universal role endowed them with the most sacred of sacred entrances directly into the Human soul. Such an advantage necessarily dictates ....dictates what!? - insisted, what appeared to be the lawyer for the Monsters (the previously observed order of the procession had dissolved and the rancor in the 'room' became nearly palpable)!!!

Why, it dictates the whole direction of the Human Soul! Exclaimed the Demons; In Unison! No one knew until now that they were all related, tied together in some way in order to feel this point all together at the same moment! What manner of creature is this before us! Before whom? The child could feel the huge currents of sentiment abounding throughout the chamber in unison – were these creatures mentally linked somehow? For there was far more communication, innuendo, and even physical positioning, than there were audible words.

It was apparent that this meeting was being conducted with complete consideration of Humanity. There is a plane of existence where Man, Monster and Demon all walk together and encounter one another! Where the unenlightened Soul of Man is prey to the ravenous desires of Monsters and Demons: Because there is no better, no richer fabric in the known Universe; not to these eternal beings.

Thorneous could actually see that the Monsters were intimidated by the immortal confidence of the Demons. The Demons openly swaggered and flaunted their pivotal influence on mankind. Moreover, events had taken on a color resembling dynamics of some familiar relation that he could not quite recall.

The Monsters erupted. The beginning of chaos ensued! The Monsters insisted that they too played a Celestial role by forcing Man to face his nature...whereas the Demons seek to subvert it!!!!! Where is the value in that?

It was at this point that the head Demon lawyer stood, and spread his arms (although to anyone who happened to see his shadow against the wall, they were actually wings), and he proceeded (he appeared to float...) to the middle of the floor to address the entire audience.

His message was unsettling, condescending, but inescapable; "We already know that Monsters thrive, yes, in fact exist only – make no mistake - because of Human fear: You serve no Celestial role other than your own persistence and appetite. We Demons, on the other hand, give the whole merry-go-round its impetus and meaning. We Cause a human to exhibit the behavior that he does. And our most ingenious circumstance is that we disappear when the time comes to either explain or pay for said behavior:

And they never see this!!!

If any human is first so brave, then, so insightful, and so true, as to interrogate himself as to the origins of his behavior (this must be done in an atmosphere of accepting responsibility – not placing blame), only then does he enter the stage where he can begin to grow wings, become light as air, and become immune to the venom that festers on the horizon of the world in which the Demons Live!!!!

Thorneous could feel the unspoken scalding reaction of the monsters…until suddenly…

"I can kill any MAN" shouted a Monster from the crowd.

Demon -

"Yes, you can kill them, but you cannot change them." Responded the Demon lawyer (Thorneous was unconsciously assigning roles to these entities – it made the encounter easier to follow).

The Demon leaned his head back, an irrepressible smile spread across his face. He was clearly enjoying all that rapture could afford him. And, he repeated, mockingly:

"You can kill any MAN! I cannot tell you how many times I have left an unsuspecting, confused and otherwise innocent man, to face the termination of his life at the hands of his 'fellow man' at the gas chamber, the gallows, and the electric chair! Does it matter who kills him, or who causes his death? Yes, I cause them to perform this task for me. We would never sink, nor could we, to the level of merely dispensing with a human being ourselves!"

"They do it for us!"

Monster -

A very young, but studious Monster answered; "You think that our abilities with humans is trivial when all a man need be is brave and true to escape your grasp! I have seen it happen often enough with my own eyes! Your only means of egress is the sewer of the soul!"

Demon –

"Yes, and every man has a sewer within his soul…"

Sensing the pursuit of omniscience on the part of the Demons "We will not submit to this judgment!!!" shouted the monsters – their scholarship thus exhausted!

"That would be our annihilation!! Without susceptible Humans, we would be left in a world attempting to squeeze water from Stones!!" Although this is not what the Demon lawyer proclaimed, fear never embraces logic, and the Monsters raged on.

"Yes you would!!" replied the Demons.

"It is not enough," thundered a strange, small, but very old Monster. As he rose from his seat far in the back of the cavern, and made his way to the middle of the floor: the center of attention. He was wrapped in ancient garb, very long, and it appeared to be of medieval origin. His utter confidence exuded from his very stride as he took the floor front and center.

"You all underestimate the gifts that mankind possesses! I have seen over the centuries, some of their kind stand tall against Monsters in their villages. I have even seen some stand even at greater heights against the invisible invasion that you Demons always prefer!!! Proving them to be men not only of strength, but of subtle insight and perseverance as well!!! You ALL underestimate your food source! Have any of you ever considered that they could in fact prevail in the end over both of us?"

With this proclamation, ALL parties in session became inflamed!! What had been the return to an ordered procession sank into a tempestuous display of rancor and acid.

Just then, transfixed by the encounter occurring before his eyes, the boy did not even feel the sneeze building up in his nasal cavities until it had extirpated itself. The noise caught the full attention of ALL.

The focus of the entire chamber swiveled in the direction of the chest with the momentum of a planet changing its orbit. Instantly there was a rush of flying fury around the chest as it was thrust open and the child was savagely grasped and lifted from his hiding place.

MONSTER -

"A HUMAN…A CHILD! Invading these sacred proceedings!!" Instantly the creature, Thorneous knew not whether Demon or Monster, opened its voracious mouth to reveal shining blades for teeth that were immediately directed to Thorneous's throat.

BOY -

"Wait!" shouted the boy. "This session is not concluded! Do you Monsters not see that you are the result of the invasion of a Human by a Demon? That is how Monsters are created!"

Stunning silence was soon followed by a deep and concerned murmur that spread throughout the room. The boy had hit an acute nerve with this crowd that was so recently embroiled in a contest to determine…determine what? We may never know.

BOY -

"Don't you see? Monsters are created by Demons that invade a human soul. That means that Monsters ARE Demons…you are all related! Why did the Demons not tell you that!!!???"

The room became so quit as to remind one of death itself. Almost imperceptively, the Monsters had shifted their position to surround the boy, as if to insure the completion of his story.

MONSTER -

"So, the Demons knew this all along, and would feign tell us that there is really a cycle involved. No, instead, the Demons seek to profess superiority! Why would you do this? Demons are NOT superior to Monsters!"

DEMON -

"We did not mention it because there is no means of return. Once a Demon invades a human they become an eternal monster. There is no way to quench the appetite for invading humans. There is no return and there is no resistance to invading humans. It is almost as if the humans are in control by virtue of their very appeal. Their souls contain the most desirable sustenance in the Universe. And, we know, because we watched and waited from the Very Beginning"

DEMON -

"But he has heard secrets hidden from mankind for centuries!!! He must be killed!!"

This did nothing to distract or quell the mounting fury among the Monsters.

Now the boy knew he had but one more chance to escape, and he must exercise his advantage now.

BOY -

"Please, put me down, I have an even more momentous revelation to share with you."

Now, the Monsters, having heard the most momentous revelation thus far, obliged, eager to hear more. And the Demons, actually shaken with the unexpected exposure of their less than honorable treatment of their relatives, found themselves actually frozen with fear that this child, this mere human creature, had even more to reveal!

The Monster put the boy down. The Monsters had unconsciously increased their shift into a defensive group position surrounding the boy.

Boy –

"Now, bring that single candle close to me and I will show you ALL the greatest of all knowledge you have been missing."

The candle was brought to him.

The boy instantly blew the candle out, throwing the entire room into total darkness and anger. The Monsters were still extremely agitated by being mislead for millennium, the Demons in a rage that a human child had been the informant, and in the terrible blind fight that followed, the boy crawled up the 'stairs' and out between the roots into daylight. They could not follow him.

The few that tried to retrieve the boy were blinded by the light of the smiling, guardian sun, for it was now daylight, and the boy raced home with pockets containing a small selection of treasures.

THE END

3433 3rd Ave South

By Kenneth G. Gary

Prelude

Can you actually enjoy tales of fright and horror with no consequences? Is it not tempting fate to supply the dark side with attention, enlivening the power therein?

- A victim

Once upon a time…

As a child, we lived in a house in the Midwest with a basement, first floor, upstairs bedrooms, and a one-room attic.

The road to the basement consisted of five short stairs to a small landing, where there was a door to the outside. But, after turning the corner to the left, it was followed by fifteen stairs, with nothing on the sides (on the ground, you could walk under the stairs), descending all the way down to the bottom. On the wall to the left along the stairway, some five feet away, there were the remnants of what used to be shelves, where old unidentifiable cans and boxes, seemed to go to just die. And, the stairs themselves had no railing; support consisted of evenly place 2x6 beams; if it were not for the collection of junk underneath them, and our abhorrence of even looking under there, there is no telling what may have been discovered. It was an overall foreign area secured by cobwebs; dank, colorless floor and walls, and dim 'stuff' that seemed to have been there forever.

My father reclaimed a portion of our unfinished basement for civilization. He was industrious and installed wood paneling along the stone cellar walls to the far right of the bottom of the staircase, flawlessly symmetric tiles upon the base cement floor, and a dropped ceiling hiding the aging beams overhead. When one reached the bottom of the stairs, there were still several yards of dark territory to traverse before entering the modernized section to the right of the staircase. Once there, where civilization extended lengthwise to the right and left of this third of the basement, the TV was placed in the most distant corner to the left of this 'good section', which drew me and my siblings there to watch our favorite monster movies; the safe wood paneling and tiles banished the fear and for a time and took us far away from the danger zone nearby; we just knew we were completely safe.

A direct left at the bottom of the stairs meant entering darkness of irrecoverable depths.

But my father's time was limited, the entire jungle was not conquered, only about one third of it on the right side at the bottom of the stairs, and, after the show, we still had to navigate a short distance through the unfinished part of the basement in order to ascend the stairway and escape that section of the basement which the horror movies thus enjoyed had now imbued with the certainty of something lurking out there.

In point of fact, I encountered the worst fate possible when I fell asleep one night, having been originally accompanied by my siblings and father, only to awaken alone. It was utterly cold and dark. In those days the television screen displayed a Native American with a full war bonnet of feathers against a background of indecipherable concentric circles and numbers; but it meant that the station had ended broadcasting for the night, and there was no one down there but me.

Seized with panic visited by the realization that in spite of the *safe zone,* where I currently sat, there was a zone of unfathomable dread between the stairs and me. And I could sense the horrific glee and anticipation with which the creatures awaited my attempt to escape my island prison. For some reason, the area my father had secured in this wilderness repelled them. But they knew I had to cross their territory to return to the living world, the world upstairs, inhabited by true human beings.

Terror, knowing no boundaries, swept through my being. I knew I could not spend the remainder of the night in the basement, in the company of sepulchral images cast by old dressers, shovels and mounds of other unnamed artifacts inhabiting basements -*and why is everything the same colorless hue?* I had to get up the stairs.

To this day I do not distinctly recall the details of my escape. But I had to escape because they would eventually penetrate the boundary of civilization and I would be doomed forever. No doubt I probably ran for my life, and set myself aflight upon the stairs, bounding three or four at a time – and, in my mind at least, there had to be hungry hands from under the stairs clutching at my feet - until I reached the top and burst through the basement door into the safety of the kitchen.

I do recall, upon looking over my shoulder to measure the success of my escape, that I vaguely perceived a pair of luminous, red eyes. They did not appear to be part of any corporeal entity; there was no bodily outline to which they could belong; yet they were there. They were right at the bottom of the stairs, lamenting my escape, and marking my very existence for a later rendezvous. No matter, I was occupied with securing my entrance back into the world of light.

Thereafter, I always selected a seat positioned to insure that I would not be the last person left in the basement at the termination of the movie. On occasion I had to watch the end of the movie from afar, being closest to the stairs. But I never allowed myself to be left alone down there again.

Our endemic relation with horror did not end there. There was also the attic.

Attics are such that at some point under the roof, one that is slanted, there is a vertical wall in place that meets the ceiling. Beyond this wall, all the way to where the roof slopes and contacts the floor, there is a sizeable crawl space. Just above the stairs descending from the attic, there was a very small room, behind a most ominous door, leading to the crawl space that circled the entire attic.

I often lay awake, utterly fearful of what monsters must lurk within that crawl space, and how they must have been designing my doom once asleep. And, they had to be there; as surely as mold grows in dark wet places, these are the places they gravitate towards.

And I had to sleep up there.

One morning the door to the small room was cracked open. I know I did not do this, as I was terrified of the entire area I would never have opened the door. But, the door, again, was just above the stairs that I had to descend. Fortunately it was morning, and in the absence of the dark power of the night, I forced myself to attempt to close the door in order to go downstairs. As I grasped the doorknob I made the mistake of peeking inside – for the aperture was only several inches wide; and all my suspicions were true. All the characters of fear and terror found only in dreams did inhabit this place. I saw nothing; I could simply sense it.

Attempting to pull the door closed, I found unmistakable resistance. This occasioned no small alarm within my chest. Further, the knob turned, with force, in my hand, not of my own accord. Something had a hold from the other side! I could not see inside but the ghastly incident was unmistakable! I released the knob as if aflame and fled down the stairs praying that I was not pursued and captured by whatever creatures of the night lay within.

But these are fears of youth, and I eventually did grow up into an adult life

Professionally, my life became marked by constant travel, hotels, rental cars, and in a strange way; people I would never see again after this trip (were they real? Are they still alive?). It invests a certain unreality into the world – into one's very life.

As the years progressed, with my mother still living there, alone now, the city concluded that they intended to buy the entire city block where our house was located. And it was just a matter of time. The city government at the time had decided that they needed to destroy every house on my block, along with the high school across the street (actually it was closer to an alley and it was behind our house), in order to build 'something else'.

The house we grew up in, five siblings, and myself is now gone.

I often joked with my friends whom I had grown up with that the houses placed in what used to be the track and field training ground for us, are going to host us running laps through their house as ghosts.

However, there was one occasion before the demolition where I visited my mother, the sole inhabitant, in order to assist an electrician survey some phenomenon requiring access to the basement.

There was some extraordinary anomaly in the billing for the month, an anomaly that amounted to one hundred times the usual billing amount.

I scheduled the visit to my mothers house between necessary professional travel which never seemed to abate. Upon arriving, as I exited the generic white rental car, my first appraisal of the house was of ominous portent. The building itself exuded something that can only be likened to the visual effect conferred by heat rising and the concomitant out-of-focus character it endows the objects of visions pursuit.

The electrician was waiting on the porch, and I walked up the stairs from the blvd, along the sidewalk to the house, and up the stairs to the porch. We introduced ourselves and I knocked on the door as he expressed he had already done, repeatedly, for the last 15 minutes. My knock was answered by a door that was not fully closed to begin with, and it gave way to immediate entrance.

The electrician was of a jolly character. He followed me inside with complete comfort. His job was sufficiently interesting, he relished apprising others with 'whatcha got here is …' type of analysis, and, he had seen a lot in his time. He had crawled through small apertures (this part of his tale was belied by his corpulence), over broken brick strewn condemned buildings, and he was intrepid in performing his duties.

Once inside, I led the electrician to the basement stairway. By the time we arrived at the head of the stairs, I was quite cautiously, behind him, pointing the way to the cellar. For a moment I felt an urge to see the room downstairs where we had spent so many enjoyable evenings watching horror movies, but I easily resisted and simply flicked the first light switch at the top of the stairs for the electrician. He proceeded, armed with an industrial strength flashlight and the confidence of having entered countless dark basements in the past.

Meanwhile, I sat and visited with my mother, who never was at a loss of topics to discuss. Soon thereafter, I heard the electrician thundering up the stairs in obvious haste. I ran to the head of the stairs to meet him to find a face that had become a ghastly white, and eyes that held a barely controlled terror; He too had seen the eyes down there that I had seen those many years before!

Silently, never removing his widened eyes from mine, he quickly produced a summary sheet, shoved it into my hand and immediately sought escape through the front door without ceremony or professional courtesy. I in turn closed the door to the basement, and locked it.

While this encounter was not lost on me, I returned to sit with my mother and discuss the details of the electricians visit. We quickly concluded this issue would best be pursued at a higher level. With the business direction addressed, my mother proceeded to describe a distinct uneasiness about the house. She mentioned having heard conversations in some of the rooms, while just outside the door. Not just any conversations, but conversations she knew had actually taken place before, as though they were being replayed.

Some of these conversations she described I recognized as well. There was an occasion with one of my older sisters failing to meet curfew. There was a far more ancient incident involving myself when I attempted to hide one of my shoes to avoid attending gymnasium the following day. It was an incident with harrowing manifestations, but, the dialogue now played itself through in my mind as well; exactly as it had been those many years before.

The most astonishing fact of all was that she was certain that some areas of the house, that had fallen into debilitating disrepair, had somehow become repaired through no effort or direction on her part. At first she attributed it to support from the church she belonged too. They were known to perform such supportive acts unbidden, and, in time, one becomes accustomed to forgetfulness. But, she did not recollect hearing any of the necessary associated noise that would accompany such considerable endeavors. In the end, the facts did not add up to what would be the necessary signs of their arrival with equipment, workmen, and so forth.

I know that she thought that I considered her observations to be simply the disjointed observations of an 'old person'. I did not think that at all, her sentience was remarkably intact, but I could not convince her of it. By the time I departed for the hotel, since it was proximal to the airport and the flight I was committed to was at dawn the following morning – in addition to the need to return the rental car. Still, I could not dismiss the events I felt I had experienced that day.

In the end, the exigencies of life have a way of sanding down these uneven surfaces, rendering unto life a flat texture that no longer references exceptional events.

One day there was a business trip that took me to Chicago. I had visited this client before and felt a considerable degree of excitement about the return trip. It was one of those 'good fits' for both sides. The meetings progressed exceptionally well; my goals were easily conveyed and perceived, granting an overall sense of comfort to all in attendance.

Afterwards, I returned to my hotel, in which I was fortunate enough to have secured all my favorite accoutrements the night before: a great view of Lake Michigan from downtown Chicago, a broad, expansive room and, not one but several large scenic windows, thus abating the constant threat of claustrophobia I suffered from. Upon reflection, it was far more likely that the horror experienced in the basement of our now nonexistent house, was a manifestation of my claustrophobia and behaviors surrounding the affliction, than any real source for my fears.

My mind was alive with business possibilities as I strolled through the luxurious lobby to the front desk to check for any messages or deliveries. The attendant behind the desk welcomed me with a knowing smile, though this was the first time I had ever seen him. Usually, and again, I had visited this client often; this concierge desk was usually occupied by the ever-effulgent Felix, who always had the latest news on the jazz and other functions citywide. Felix was attentive to the preferences of all his regulars.

I instituted various queries in the direction that Felix would have already summarized and portrayed by now. This attendant delivered inept and even careless responses to my questions from behind his opaque, dark glasses. There was in fact a distinct character of malevolence that seeped through a crack in his presentation. I began to get that circular feeling often yielded by phone systems that do not allow any progress towards ones goal no matter what key selections you decide on. With that, I simply thanked him, unperturbed, and I turned to walk away and enjoy what was bound to be a glorious sunset over the lake before dinner.

I had not progressed three paces before the unhelpful attendant casually offered the viewing of an old-fashioned horror movie that was beginning shortly. I turned to look at him, inquire as to which of the classics it actually was. To my surprise, he had removed his glasses to reveal something vaguely familiar in his more than slight red-eyed gaze (he looked like he suffered, acutely, from lack of sleep). He assured me it would be one to my liking.

I thanked him, and, anxious to enjoy my extraordinary room, I turned and took the elevator to my elegant abode for the evening. I turned on the television, ordered room service, and began to have rich recollections of this particular black and white era horror movie that I had always enjoyed. The steak was perfectly rendered, the mashed potatoes gloriously seasoned, and I had a robust appetite to enjoin them.

I determined to not have my exalted state interfered with and the laptop stayed within the case, the cell turned off, and I sat joyfully immersed in the movie that was like family to me, and the food – so delicious as to elicit audible grunts of satisfaction.

There really is no accounting for all the effects of travel; the stress of schedule, the anxiety of reservations, standing in the lines; placing ones very life in the hands of smiling strangers. Before too long, I could tell that with the food, and, admittedly, the egotistical comfort afforded by imminent business success, I relaxed and allowed sleep to envelop me.

I woke to find myself in utter darkness. It was cold. And it was dark. It took several moments for my vision to acclimate to the low light. To my utter horror the scene before me was impossible! This must be a dream! I had been lying on the sofa in the basement and the TV had the Native American on the screen with the same indecipherable background as when I was a child. But this house no longer exists! And these channels are now cable; they never go off!

Forcing myself to look towards the stairs, which in my youth had so often symbolized a passage through Hades itself in order to remain in this world, I saw the owner of those gleaming red eyes perceived long ago when we actually lived 'here'. He was no longer deep within the shadows. He was right at the entrance to the stairs.

'How did I get here?' I blurted.

The confrontation afforded 'him' a chance to speak.

'Why, you, and your siblings created me with your constant flirtations with fear and dread. I was 'asleep', shall we say – *for no one really knows where they are from* - but your persistent, importunate calls to me brought me here.'

In spite of my complete horror, the logic thus expressed bore some measure of clarity; barely above thorough insanity, but it was a plateau; and escape was out of the question.

'What calls?' I asked, with a quivering child's voice, seeking mercy and any chance of leniency at the same time.

I noticed that the neat symmetrical floor tiles began to bubble and curl at the edges, I could hear the snapping sound of the soothing wood paneling on the walls as it cracked and fell to the floor revealing an irregular gray dungeon surface behind ...the ceiling tiles began to fall to the floor, smoldering with the promise of flames.

He responded, smiling; 'The calls born of your tempting powers that you have no understanding of. Nothing is insignificant. Your very attention is the most formative power in this world. And now, you have given it to me. Did you not recognize me in the hotel?'

With that said, the red eyes, followed by impenetrable darkness, came closer and closer; easily invading what had always been the safe zone in our basement, and sealing my doom.

The End

"The Hospital"

By Kenneth G. Gary

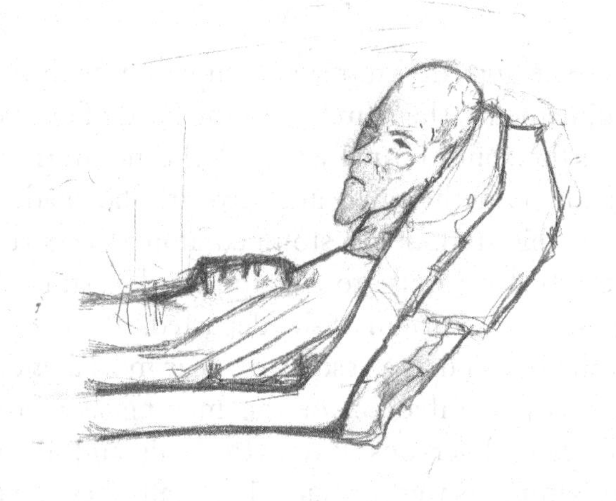

Prelude

Imminent death lay in the next bed: 'Ask not for whom the bell tolls…it tolls for thee.'

- John Donne

Once upon a time…

The man in the next bed, reduced by severely advanced age and unyielding pain, cried out that night. I could hear, no, I could sense, in the sound of her footsteps that the night nurse thus summoned by his cries, harbored ill intent. To be sure, though I could barely turn my head to watch the bigger than life shadows reflected on the curtain partitioning our respective areas; there was no mistake that her vehemence was given free reign to stalk the occasion, unmitigated, as she forcefully tossed him about.

Under her breath was unrepressed acidity. She grumbled, and very nearly growled, as she repositioned him with complete intolerance. Tossing him to and fro as an imprisoned criminal for whom there was no recourse but to suffer the battering. It caused him to cry even louder in pain and indignation.

I was helpless to assist the situation. In fact, I lie with bated breath lest she discover that I had witnessed her assault and felt behooved to silence me also. Self-preservation dictated that I feign sleep and ignorance of the event; I was as helpless as a mortally wounded victim myself.

Finally, as she appeared to reach completion with the necessary positional adjustments, she marched to the head of our beds to what I thought of as the 'control panel' where all the monitoring equipment was located for both this man and myself. She made some final adjustments at this station and stomped along the curtain towards the end of the beds in route to exit the ward, casting an image of malevolence upon the curtain as she departed.

I was in the hospital as a result of a near mortal encounter with viral meningitis: An infection of the meningeal membrane that surrounds the central nervous system; the brain and spinal cord. The concomitant symptoms were excruciating headaches and debilitating fever. In fact, upon being seized by the malady initially, I could only crawl from my bedroom into the hallway in front of the bathroom hoping to be discovered by one of my roommates who would provide some aid.

I was soon discovered and bodily lifted and transported a short distance to Boston City Hospital.

I suffered unabated pain throughout the nights and days, I know not how long, in spite of the purported strength of the painkillers. In fact, in that strange way that dreams are orchestrated by sensory input, I often had dreams of being bound in ancient chambers of torture.

Images sponsored by my interminable pain, no doubt. In such a condition, I could but watch the larger than life silhouettes upon the curtain; the depiction of a ghastly scene of abuse and crime. And most miserable of all, myself; praying, not for the victim, but that I should not follow him in her trail of torment.

Strangely enough, as vulnerable as I was, I could not help but notice that although the night nurse, whom I had never actually seen, cast a silhouette on the curtain that was very attractive in spite of her seeming ill temper. She was tall, a little thin, but well proportioned.

The doctors increased the dose of pain medications several times to the limits that no one was willing to exceed, all with no effect.

Dr "How do you feel?"

"This pain is unbearable."

Dr. "It is a bit baffling, the source of this pain. The viral meningitis alone should not cause this. Fever, yes, but the pain…"

"It is not getting any better."

A feverish mind is a suspicious source of record, but, I do recall that, seemingly days later, a doctor decided to perform a spinal tap in the event that the infection had accelerated the production of CSF (Cerebral Spinal Fluid) which itself could contribute to the pain in a significant fashion.

He performed the spinal tap. After which he cautioned me…

Dr. "You must remain horizontal. What we have done is remove some of the Cerebral Spinal Fluid from your Central Nervous System. Now, your brain needs to float in this fluid else you will experience extreme pain nearly immediately."

"How long will I be like this?"

Dr. "It differs with different people. Your temperature may persist for a while. But we may have eliminated the symptom of the viral infection which caused the build up of the fluid, which is worse as you know because excess fluid is constantly painful where low fluid is only painful if you raise your head allowing it to leave the brain case, like any fluid would."

Dr. "Just stay on your back. You are young and it will resolve itself naturally from this point."

The doctor's suspicion was correct, but the 'cure' was not without consequence. As promised, while lying horizontal, I was now afforded comfort and freedom from pain. However, should I rise, to relieve myself for instance, it would occasion the most frightful torture that would render me immobile within three paces, or 3 seconds; whichever should occur first.

I was able to observe my neighbor earlier that day because the orderly had left the separating curtain open. The man was of unusual length. This was discernable even as he lay in the bed. Even with his knees bent his feet were up against the low horizontal bedpost, almost exerting a grip upon it, and when he made what appeared to be a most prodigious effort to raise his hand, there was complete surprise at how far down the length of the bed under the cover his hand actually was. But his face, or rather his profile, projected a very large and hooked nose, deeply sunken eyes, and his mouth (maxillary and mandibular) protruded slightly, albeit noticeably, in a canine like fashion. An extremely wan and pallid character pervading his body accompanied all this. In places there were large sickly blue blotches covering his exposed forearms. This man was morbidity incarnate, and, forgive my intolerance, but he was a sickening sight to behold.

The next morning brought cleansing rays of the sun, evaporating all lingering midnight shadows, and, perhaps, last night never happened at all. But still, the old man in the next bed was as hideous as ever, even in his sleep. Through the thin, institutional bed covers, one could easily perceive that there was a resemblance to a somewhat tangled and oddly positioned fossil that had been pressed against a rock for millennia. And I actually heard, in a distant corner of my soul, the wish that she had accomplished his demise last night and he would no longer be here to vex me today.

On occasion, during the night, though I could not move more than a violin in its case, I could gain report of what was occurring through the length of the ward by the shadows on the distal wall. It appeared there were at least a dozen beds in this ward; all positioned the same as mine. The window above my head heralded the sun every morning. Thus it must face the east. As the ward fell into darkness every evening, the lights by each bedside afforded me a shadowy newscast of local events upon the opposite western wall.

Although my appetite was rapaciously returning, every meal became the very bane of my existence as each attendant, no matter how often I insisted on the matter, they would leave the curtain drawn back. This left me to witness the horror of what was very nearly a mummy next to me, attempting to nourish his already lifeless body. In health, we consume meals with vigor; for him, in spite of being spoon fed, the food itself had no desire to engage in the process; it ran down his face in hopeless abhorrent tracks; almost as if repelled by his imminent death.

My appetite vanished.

When night finally arrived, I dreamed of a woman, in front of me with beautiful stark black flowing hair. It was a perfect match to her glowing black eyes. She was wearing a long, black, one- piece formal dress circa 1700, as though she had been entertaining guests that evening. It was the kind of dress they wore that demanded the woman's waist be as small as possible. And, she was entrancingly beautiful. I was walking towards her but she was walking backwards away from me. We were in a large highly adorned mansion on the second floor landing near the banister leading to a stairway. This mansion was clearly a 17th century dwelling with a magnificent chandelier just to my left over the banister.

I continued to walk towards her until her back hit the wall. There was now a huge blaze on the first floor, someone screamed, I continued to walk towards the woman. Her eyes expanded in terror as I continued. to approach her. She began to scream…

The next afternoon, lunch was a particularly special treat. My then roommates, from our nearby apartment, in a display of genuine concern, brought me a steak sub of my most favorite variety.

It is claimed that man is possessed of five senses. There are those occasions where other, not classically recognized, senses, do appear. It happens at rare moments of need, or extreme instances of distress; here, it was simply the overwhelming olfactory memory, proximity of good friends, and the possibility of escaping my immediate physical surroundings all-collaborating to bring a sense of extreme elation.

But! Before I could expect to eat at all, I asked one of my roommates, nearest the 'curtain of separation' to perform the honors of isolating my self from my disgusting neighbor that I could enjoy my meal thus secured from the outside world, with pleasure.

To my utter dismay, my friend thus assigned to draw the curtain, found that there was in fact no curtain at all on the tracks that were clearly visible on the ceiling. My friend also exhibited no recognition of the fact that the man in the next bed was hopelessly horrid. It was impossible he did not see this, yet, he simply turned back to me and shrugged his shoulders; there was no evidence in his countenance that he had just seen, and was standing next to, something completely repulsive. Conceit declined to allow the consideration that perhaps my friend simply had better manners than to complain. After all; this is a hospital. No matter; the absence of the curtain, this fateful condition ushered upon me a volcanic eruption of desperation, despair, and finally, a nearly demonic anger.

I immediately assigned the conception and execution of the crime to him: this death walker in the next bed.

This man next to me, this sepulchral frame, this caricature of life, this blue-blotched bridge between life and imminent mortality, was somehow poisoning every rare moment of brightness and joy that arose in my life.

I resolved to eliminate this problem, and have my nemesis removed at any cost; the fact that I was completely immobile notwithstanding.

When the night nurse arrived she stopped to read my chart and check on me. I stiffened up with apprehension. When she sat on the bed beside me, seductively, I relaxed. She had ink black hair, tightly rolled into a bun in the back and a crisp white nurses hat on her head. Her eyebrows, long lashes and pupils were equally black; all combining with her stark paleness to produce an almost frightening beauty.

Nurse "Come, look at the stars from the hallway window. It will soothe you. I promise." Her smile was utterly entrancing.

"I can't, stand up, I had a spinal tap…".

Nurse "Trust me. Take my hand." She said, leaning over me, her radiance increasing.

I took her hand. I almost did not even feel myself pulling down the covers and was nearly on my feet when I remembered! I braced myself for vicious pain that was sure to come…

But there was none.

Nurse "Just do not release my hand, you will be fine."

We walked slowly out of the ward. The hospital was quiet this time of night. We walked down the corridor, I made sure to keep her hand as we were now so far from the bed that should the pain come I would be in crushing agony before I could make it back.

We stood in silence together, holding hands. The stars in the sky were indeed glorious. More so than I have ever noticed before. I turned to share that joy with her but I was stunned at how vaguely familiar she looked.

I don't remember walking back...

That night I dreamt of walking slowly down a moist, warm, old road lined with huge trees sprouting ancient limbs that arched across the road creating a cavernous effect. It was nighttime, and I instinctively knew I was not in the current time, rather, it was a very old time. Unlike my current debilitated situation in real life, I easily began to bound down the lane nearly free of all gravitational influence when suddenly the object of my pursuit appeared.

She was young but physically mature. She wore a very long, black dress, with a white apron fixed upon it. As I swooped into range of contact, for now a near flight like capacity had been added to my repertoire, I was shocked when she wheeled around to face me just as it seemed a dozen men assailed me with ropes and strange, brilliantly gleaming objects that were blinding in the moonlight.

Unlike the constrictions of most dreams where we find ourselves moving in slow motion, making our attempts at escape tortuous, this dream imbued me with power. So much so that the attackers were not only repelled but I easily inflicted mortal wounds upon several of them as we struggled in the dark on that dusty, ancient road. Others fled in desperate fear. The last thing I recall was grabbing my prey, the young girl, by the throat, and witnessing, in her eyes and her complete immobility, the note of mortal finality that grasped her very soul.

She dropped the blinding object that she expected to secure her salvation.

The following morning, I could remember no details of my dream but the entire character of it lingered on. I knew that hospital staff is directed to insure patient's sleep by liberal application of medication. I just had no idea that they would produce such fantastic dreams.

I had somehow forgotten the Dr's orders to stay prone. I started to sit up and the merciless pain engulfed me almost immediately.

I managed to convince one of the lethargic attendants that I needed to have the curtain replaced. He nodded, gave me some excuse about needing to contact housekeeping and engineering, after which the deed could be accomplished.

I was elated to find that my next meal was, once again, delivered from the real world, where food has flavor and appeal. However, to my dismay, the attendant could not succeed in getting the newly replaced curtain to actually move in its tracks, thus leaving me exposed to this mockery of life in the next bed with his appetite vaporizing powers.

I flew into such a rage that I momentarily forgot my own condition and attempted to rise; only to find the stern marshal of pain assault every nerve in my body, rendering me a retching, pitiable mass of protoplasm.

This cadaver next to me will not continue to inflict such disturbance upon my life…

That night, the dreams returned. I call them dreams for lack of a better term; for they were of a character that left me sweating, exhausted, and thoroughly convinced that they were real until I returned to this world where there is sunshine. Nevertheless, in this dream I …could not tell definitely where I was. It is curious that locale was even a question, which made me realize there was a certain continuity pervading these 'dreams'. So much so that I had even began to expect a certain consistency.

It was dark, and I was restrained. From the darkness there emerged a vast crowd of people, carrying torches, their approach was drenched with trepidation, and rightly so, for restraining me had been futile for a long time. Finally from the rear of the crowd, as they parted to allow his entrance, there was some figure of great pontifical significance that walked resolutely towards me. He wore stern black clothing, a long jacket with white ruffles at the cuffs and collar. He approached me with a large ancient book open in his arms. He was chanting some words or phrases that upon reaching my ears, seemed to burn my very soul.

As he came closer and closer, I thought that these strangely powerful words would render me into pieces if he continued with this painful onslaught…I felt myself shriek with a pain that echoed throughout the heavens, and my call was answered by a mindless but dedicated contingent of morbid humans that arrived just in time to engineer my freedom from the specially constructed stocks.

In my freedom, with the strength of the night, I reigned my mortal vengeance upon this crowd who dared attempt to restrain me.

The next morning, the doctor on his rounds noted that I actually should have been further advanced in my recovery by now. While I was still captivated by the dream, I actually agreed with this assertion and assigned the fact to the lack of food, or rather, my inability to consume such with the vision of death lying in the next bed.

The doctor glanced at the next bed, then back at me, with a look of complete bewilderment – as if he did not know what to say next. I continued on, expressing how ridiculous it was to expect me to eat with that drooling, sagging, bag of near death visible to me the whole time. The doctor just hastily wrote some additional notes in his pad, assured me that everything would be all right, and quickly departed.

That night, I determined that I would mimic the sounds of this mortuary bound man next to me, such that the nurse, with her last string of patience gone, would finally rid me of this unholy nuisance.

It did not take long to make her march into the ward, and there was no mistake of her fatefully resounding footsteps and the promise of reprisal they carried. As she approached our area of the ward, I deftly quitted my fake groans and whines, fully expecting that she would attack the usual suspect with all the fervor she now possessed.

To my utter surprise, she entered my side of the curtain, and forcibly grabbed me by the neck, lifted my head to remove the pillow underneath. Then she forced my head back against the bed, planted the pillow against my face, from the nose down, blocking every chance of respiration to continue.

And her hair! Long black hair hung down over me. Her black eyes gleaming. I knew she looked familiar – yes, I had seen her in my dream!

I could only mumble in horror at the failure of my plan, when, I happened to turn my attention to the screen that had separated me from the near dead man next to me, and he was standing; Yes Standing! His silhouette appeared to be muscular and well over seven feet tall! This had to be a true depiction of his frame as he was standing so frighteningly close to the curtain that there was no possibility of the exaggerations that a more distant position could have offered. And even through the flat gray of a silhouette I could detect a triumphant smile on his face, as he gracefully, mockingly, raised his hand and pointed to the IV next to my bed.

Looking up, though the world was becoming dim, I could see that my IV was not supplying me with saline and medication as expected, rather, the tube was filled with blood. My blood; which was being routed from my side to his, thus nourishing him as it debilitated me!

This creature was Nosferatu! Count Dracula! A Vampire! There was no mistaking his smile as his silhouette walked gracefully along the curtain and out of the ward with a stride of strength and utter confidence.

And, yes! The dreams! They were not dreams at all, they were his memories. Memories of *when he turned* this very nurse: of times when mankind attempted to confine his rapacious cancer, his intractable evil; these dreams were his memories of attempts by the church to convert him to the light.

For me, the world was quickly turning dark…

The White Dog

By Hedy M. Gray

Prelude

I always liked to hear the stories my Grandmaw told. Some were funny. Some were scary, but that was okay because I was safe in her lap. Mostly I'd fall asleep before the end anyway and have to depend on Jimmy to tell me his version. Of course the re-telling was often incorrect or misunderstood by me and/or Jimmy. That's how Grandmaw's story about the white dog got all mixed up. Still it became my favorite story.

- Hedy M. Gray

See, it all started because I had the perfect hiding place. Nobody could find me. I was little so I just balled all up in the swing hanging from the tree. At first I could hear everyone running all around and laughing. Having fun. They all found everyone else. But not me. Nobody found me. I just listened and enjoyed all the commotion going on.

It was loads of fun for a while until Mary Beth started yelling and screaming hysterically, "it's getting late!"

I didn't pay her no mind. Jimmy said she always over acted anyway.

Jimmy was right next to me, almost under me and the swing for a while. He never looked up. He never saw me. Then he too started yelling, "Come on y'all, game over! Game over!" I saw everybody gather around the base except me. Then he started swearing and threatening me with bodily harm if I didn't stop playing.

I heard them talking: "Maybe she went home, Jimmy..." "Naw, she'd never leave without me..." "Maybe she's lost... maybe, maybe, maybe..." But no one said I won.

They started talking about how I didn't play fair and on and on.

I just started sucking my thumb smugly thinking how they were just a bunch of sore losers. I had won the game! I was so happy. So proud of myself. I never won, but this time I did! I won the game. I was going to let them act a fool a little longer before jumping out...

Then I heard the dreaded warning: Someone yelled, "LIGHTS OUT!!" The code meaning the sun was going down fast.

I looked out from under my cover of leaves.

It was too late.

I had waited too long.

I saw the sun was almost gone. I started to panic as I heard bare feet flopping, moving the dirt as they all started running hurriedly down the path. I un-balled my body and tried to get out of the swing. Leaves were falling everywhere. My shirt was stuck on the rope knot. In my panic I could not get out of my hiding place.

I started to cry, "Jimmy, Jimmy! Help me! I'm stuck in the swing!"

I heard him swearing as he tried to get me out of the swing, "if I'm late 'cause of you... you'll pay for this! You heard us tell you game over..."

I heard my shirt rip. Jimmy lifted me up and I felt my feet hit the ground as Jimmy fell on his behind. Then I saw him start to run. I started to cry again, louder. Jimmy came back huffing and steaming mad.

He grabbed my hand and muttered, "Come on cry baby!"

I cried harder. Jimmy got madder and jerked me faster and harder. My feet barely touched the ground. I cried more. Then all of a sudden Jimmy stopped dead still. I bumped right into him.

What on earth could be the matter? We needed to hurry home. We were gonna be late. I looked at Jimmy and was about to cry again and complain.

I saw Jimmy was pointing up the road. The trees on both sides of the road should have made the path almost black, but I saw there was a strange light as I followed his trembling finger. And I saw it.

A white dog was sitting in our path. Nobody here had a white dog that I knew of... a white dog was bad luck. Jimmy told me so. One day a long time ago he had said, "Grandmaw told me a white dog is bad luck if it crosses your path."

"What'll we do?" I asked Jimmy holding his hand tighter.

"Be quiet!" Jimmy said in a quiet shout. His voice was shaking. His hand was shaking. I began to shake, too. It was getting darker all around except for the strange light from the white dog.

I looked up the road. It was the longest, darkest road in the world. We had to walk the road to get home. We were always supposed to be back in the house before dark but we were having so much fun today that the time crept up on us.

The truth became clear, I knew we would not be home on time.

Jimmy would blame me. I knew he would. He always did.

I started to blame the white dog, "he'll make us late. Why don't he move?"

"Just be quiet, would ya."

We stood watching the clean white dog. He was not mangy or hungry looking. His coat looked all curly and clean.

Trying to gain courage Jimmy started to whisper to me, "he belongs to somebody... he's well kept and looks friend..."

Jimmy's talking was cut off because just then the white dog lay down as if relaxing. We stepped back in unison and looked at each other alarmed.

"What'll we do now, Jimmy?" I asked.

"I don't know, dummy," Jimmy said, "just be quiet."

I started to whimper.

"Stop it!" Jimmy shouted.

The white dog's ears perked up and he sat back up. Jimmy pulled me back a little more.

Everything was quiet.

There were no bird sounds.

The wind was not blowing.

Everything was still and quiet.

I was afraid. I looked at Jimmy waiting for him to tell me what to do.

But Jimmy did not utter a sound.

All I heard was his shaky breathing.

I thought about all the ghost stories Jimmy told me he'd heard from Grandmaw.

I started to see eyes on the trees. I heard a woof howl. The coming darkness became shapes. I started to shake violently and cry.

As if in response to my crying the white dog got up on all four of his paws. He cocked his head to one side. He looked like he was about to walk or run away.

"He's going to charge toward us," I whispered.

"You don't know that... Be still. Be quiet. We gotta see which way he's going," Jimmy said nervously.

I heard a dog wags his tail if he's friendly. The white dog's tail was not waging. It just curled up in the air. It didn't even seem to be breathing. You couldn't even see it's eyes. The hair covered them. The white dog was perfectly still.

The white dog didn't go anywhere.

The white dog just stood there. In our way... Still.

We stood where we were. Very Still barely breathing.

It was getting darker but the white dog looked like he was shinning and the road around him was as bright as day. I looked in the sky. There were stars coming out now. The stars were twinkling like they were happy. I was not happy. I looked at Jimmy. He did not look happy. I wanted to go home. I could not go home because the darn white dog would not move.

I started to shake with fear again because it was dark... we'd get a whipping for being late... Jimmy would blame me. He wouldn't play with me all because of this darn old white dog.

The shinny white dog still would not move. I saw and heard a large wind up clock ticking away the seconds of my life.

Then for no apparent reason the white dog started slowly trotting toward us. Jimmy held me tight. He was shaking too now. Or was it just me shaking?

No. We were both shaking.

"Remember, the grownups said don't run or dogs will chase you," Jimmy whispered with a small trembling voice.

We didn't run. My feet were stuck to the road. I looked at Jimmy. His eyes were shut tight. I squeezed my eyes shut, too but, I peeked. I saw the white dog coming near. He looked like he was trotting in slow motion. I could not close my eyes again. I could not move.

The white dog looked like his teeth were ready to eat us up. He looked hungry and then he started to grin! I felt like we were going to be his dinner for sure. I imagined him chewing on our bones like our neighbor Jake's old hound dog Scooter ate left over bones. I knew we were going to die and my life flashed through my mind just like they said it would. It was a short life so I didn't see much. Tears rolled down my face thinking about all the fun I'd miss because I'd be dead.

The white dog slowly trotted towards us. Then I felt a warm breeze as the white dog trotted right through us! I turned my head and saw the white dog behind us.

I screamed. I fainted. I must have fallen down. I came to on the ground as I felt Jimmy slapping my face.

"Did you see...?" I tried to ask Jimmy.

"Come on before he comes back. He didn't cross our path he walked the same way we came from. We're safe."

"But did you see...? I began again.

"Hurry! You already made us in deep trouble," Jimmy said pulling me down the path.

We both looked back often watching the white dog slowly disappear down the path behind us. It looked like a spot light was shinning on him all the way until he vanished. Jimmy and I looked at each other and ran as fast as we could.

When we got home all sorts of people were standing on the porch.

Jimmy moaned, "we're in big trouble."

But nobody even looked at us. Pretty soon Grandmaw burst out of the screen door crying. She saw us and rushed over to hug us, "come on in and say good bye to your Grandpaw."

"We're sorry to be late but... a white dog..."

Grandmaw grabbed me, "a white dog? Oh Lord, did you see a white dog?"

"Yes ma'am but it didn't cross our path..." Jimmy said.

"What did it do, baby?"

Jimmy just hunched his shoulders and said, "nothing. Just made us late. He wouldn't move."

"The white dog walked through us..." I said.

Jimmy looked at me in disbelief.

Grandmaw fell to the ground. Uncle Benny picked her up and carried her into the house.

"Why'd you tell that lie?" Jimmy demanded.

"Didn't you see it?" I asked.

"No and neither did you."

"Didn't you feel the white dog go through us?"

"All I felt was the wind as it walked by to the other side of the road," Jimmy insisted.

All the people stayed all night talking and humming church songs.

We were quiet and napped off and on. Felt like we were in church.

The next morning we got word Uncle Benny's neighbor's wife died.

"Just dropped dead," he reported.

Finally Grandmaw came out and hugged us tight, "thank you. Thank you both. You looked death square in the face. You stopped him and he passed on by."

"But Grandmaw, we thought if a white dog crossed our path we'd have bad luck," Jimmy whined.

"So we just waited until he kept on going..." I added.

"No baby," Grandmaw said, "that's a black cat. If a black cat crosses your path you'll have bad luck. Now if you just see a white dog somebody close to you will maybe die. You stood in death's path and it seems like he got tired and passed on by."

"Oh," I said, "so death was after Grandpaw?"

"Maybe, you never know..." she said.

From then on, off and on I heard Grandmaw tell the white dog story to whoever would listen, and we were the heroes.

The white dog is my favorite story.

The Painting

By Hedy M. Gray
Kenneth G. Gary

Prelude

"Ashes to ashes..."

- Book of Common Prayer

Once upon a time...

The family was engulfed with grief. It felt as though the sun had risen one day only to illuminate desolation stretching across the face of the earth, to every corner of the horizon. There was an intolerable oppressive mood pervading all of them, and it seemed that no relief, no solace, would ever visit them again.

The very well loved Mr. Anders had passed away. He was survived by his wife, daughter and son.

In life, Mr. Cornelius Anders exuded a positive magnetic quality creating an invisible 'circle of concern' around his closely-knit family. His son Blake's best friend Ingram, to his good fortune, was included within this circle. People typically do not overtly identify those possessing such qualities, but they express themselves in that during particularly trying times, one would find oneself in audience with a person of such character, and being in complete comfort in doing so; we know instinctively with whom we can share without adverse risk.

Mr. Anders was indeed special. He could walk, safely, in neighborhoods where one's life was worth less than a dollar, completely unscathed. Not because he possessed power of resistance, rather, ill intent simply passed through him, finding no home or target at all.

Ingram was since boyhood a very close friend of the family. In fact, he was literally considered family, and the feeling was entirely mutual. Ingram and Blake Anders, the only son, were best friends since grade school.

Ingram was undeniably unique. While he could nearly see around corners, in more ways than one, his social adaptation was inept at best, and at times the source of vile ridicule from other children. It was on these occasions that Blake found himself in fist fights to protect Ingram, who simply was not capable of avoiding such incidents or meeting them when they arose. There was nothing purposeful in Ingram's behavior; he was devoid of certain given understandings that are common to most.

There was one incident that, fortunately, every witness seemed to just overlook, or somehow forget. There was a very attractive girl that Ingram had clearly developed affection for. She was not cruel, but as his advances increased, she one day impatiently scolded him; crushing his thin emergence of self identification. Later that afternoon in English class, Ingram did not attend to the in class assignment. Instead he spent 45 minutes with unearthly concentration drawing something on a blank, unlined, sheet of paper.

Near the end of class, Ingram made sure that he arose from his seat early and in making his way to the door, as he passed the girl that had wounded him far more than she could ever know, and, he held the picture in front of her. As she looked up, while gathering her notebooks, her eyes revealed a shock reverberating through her body. She was instantly physically ill and vomited immediately on her desk before everyone.

The event was heightened by the excitement of all around. The girl's brother, being in the same class was determined that Ingram had inflicted some unwelcome physical assault upon his sister. Blake again found it necessary to come to the rescue of his (brother?) dearest friend. With some shoving and raised voices, soon the teacher intervened and doused the fire. And, as often happens in youth, exaggerated circumstances simply fade away.

But not completely. Blake had paid special attention to the incident from the time Ingram arose from his seat prematurely. Blake also made special efforts to recover the paper with the apparently insidious drawing on it. Upon holding the paper up for his review he was shocked to find there was nothing on it at all – not on either side. There was no mistake, there was no other page in the vicinity. At the same time he could hear the girl exclaiming as she left the classroom, with considerable assistance, how horrible a depiction the drawing had been – obviously so, to make her physically sick. Blake looked at the paper in his hand, there was no doubt this was what Ingram had showed her; and it was completely blank, on both sides.

Blake never forgot the incident. Ingram seemed to forget it almost immediately.

Ingram had a remarkably singular artistic gift that he had shared often with this family. There were extraordinary paintings he had created all over their house – and, though unspoken, they all felt an unusual sense of warmth regarding them; these paintings, inexplicably, availed themselves of change, not stagnation - and the somber depression he now felt all around, and within, gave him an idea.

He approached Mrs. Anders, at some respectable length of time after the funeral, and vowed to paint a picture of her deceased husband that would emanate all of the memories that anyone had of Mr. Anders monumental personage. Being wrapped in complete fervor, he proposed that this was the next best thing to a living depiction of Mr. Anders.

Mrs Anders, though still in the deep trenches of grief, was so moved by the gesture itself that she assented forthwith and allowed Ingram to proceed with what she knew would be – because she knew Ingram – something more than a mere novel design. Her maternal instincts continued to operate through her own emotional turmoil, and she felt that allowing this endeavor would at least help in repairing Ingram himself in some measure. In spite of a conspicuous preternatural glow in his eye, born of the vigor accompanying his conception no doubt, she had no question that Ingram felt the loss as deeply as anyone, and art was his outlet.

The urn containing the ashes of Mr. Anders was, during this acute phase of recovery in the days immediately following the burial proceedings, a sepulchral reference that Mrs. Anders could not endure daily. She was compelled to place the urn in a tall, ornate and beautifully fitted antique glass doored cabinet in one corner of the living room. A respectful placement, though not conspicuous. Not now.

Once he envisioned his goal more clearly, Ingram, being the unbridled artist that he was, he decided that it would take three paintings to actually capture different sides of Mr. Anders properly. This really was motivated by sincere reverence, as Ingram did not have any other father than Mr. Anders himself.

But something deep within him knew that he needed something special…

On the eve in which he secured the consent to engage in his compelling endeavor, with everyone else having retired for the evening (he often saw himself out as the frequency of his visits had long dissipated any formalities), before leaving the Anders house that evening, he was drawn to the cabinet containing the urn. He had no previous knowledge that it had actually been placed there; barely perceivable behind a large framed photograph of the Anders wedding.

With arrested breath, Ingram found himself frozen in every capacity. There was something coming; his acute (and perhaps extra) senses were anchored with certainty of this fact. He stood there… waiting, until finally he heard it…

When the world returned, in genuine admiration and enthusiasm, he took the urn to his studio and began his work. The urn would not even be missed from its virtual hiding place – and Ingram would not even recall removing it from the cabinet. He carefully and lovingly introduced small quantities of the contents of the urn with his pools of paint, exulting in the fact that his beloved Mr. Anders would in a way, live on. He was determined that this product would be more than just a painting, and he gave himself over to the task completely.

Ingram attacked the work with an ardor that seldom visits man. Day and night progressed unnoticed. He ate nothing; slept not at all, and drank very little water, and this only when his thirst, and painfully parched lips, seemed to threaten his progress.

There were several occasions, he could not accurately relate whether during the day or during the night, where there was a mild wind, of sorts, that seemed to circulate throughout his studio.

It crossed his mind that he had never noticed this before, but, he attributed it to mere fatigue, and he continued with what was now his obsession. He also noticed, but would not remember, that a small pile of his father's ashes on the table, destined for the paints, was impervious to this wind – it did not blow away in spite of its exposure - as he somehow knew that it would be. Nearby papers, were, however, given to flight by this same wind – not sharing in the same reverence bestowed upon the ashes.

Ingram could not quite determine what it was, but, the paint, the brush, or both, seemed imbued with intent that was not inspired by him. His arm never tired. He was hasty and did not plan or design anything before he began. As time went on, for all of his other commonly called worldly sense's were in abeyance, Ingram became mildly unnerved with the distinct and imperious fashion in which the painting was forcing its own emergence upon the canvas, leaving him a hapless observer of a growing, ghastly production.

But Ingram had a vast artistic talent, and he braved this novel though disquieting phenomenon.

Three days later, with no food or sleep, by sunrise, he had produced three paintings. One was to remain with Ms Anders, and one for both her daughter and son; the latter, of course, being his own very best friend.

The first, and probably the most auspicious painting, showed Mr. Anders looking across a verdant terrain, with what appeared to be total absorption in the sunset. His face was possessed of a countenance of timeless ease, gentleness and appreciation of a view so full of Gods beauty. *Only man can mar gods innate beauty*, he thought.

The second painting depicted him in his workshop, because Mr. Anders spent every extra moment sawing wood and building something, whether necessary or not. Ingram captured everything from the worn character of the overalls and the weight of the tool belt to the posture of the figure in the painting whose very body language spoke of the complete attention assigned to the task before him on the workbench.

The third and last painting had him fishing. Mr. Anders had not lived a long life without learning how to relax on occasion. Even more than this, being the kind of man he was, Mr. Anders's engagement in fishing was more an act of reverence than anything else. Ingram's painting had the uncanny ability to bring this understanding to life so much so that if one stared at the painting with sufficient intent, you just might perceive the gentle rocking of the boat in concert with the generous, sun sparkled, undulating lake.

This painting surrounded Mr. Anders with the fisherman's dream day: serene water, brilliant sunshine, and you could nearly hear the birds and wind against the trees.

Ingram delivered the paintings with complete nonchalance to the Anders family that evening at dinner. He had always seemed to have no appreciation of his artistic genius himself. For him, it was closer to working ones way through some feverish assault; it was a pursuit of peace.

His body, however, was in complete recognition of the state that it was in. He ate ravenously. Mrs. Anders, sympathetically, provided, and encouraged, as much sustenance as his appetite could address.

Mrs. Anders chose to place the painting of the scene where Mr. Anders was surveying the meadow in her room. Her son, Jr., chose to adorn his room with the painting of his father fishing, as he had accompanied his father on such trips along with Ingram. Her daughter, Chanel, cheerfully adopted the painting of the workshop where she had, in her tomboy fashion, worked with her father on the very bookcase that was in the corner of her room at this very moment.

All of the paintings were cherished by the Anders family. Ingram's extreme efforts in creating them did not go unnoticed either. He dined with the family more frequently than ever. Eventually, with the passing of time, and the blessing of the paintings, the family, including Ingram, began to feel the possible return of a spring season in their lives.

One evening Mrs. Anders attended an office function. She was one of those women who owned the blessed fortune of aging very gracefully. There was a persistent suitor who attended the occasion also. And on this occasion, with the champagne, the noise, and the need to forget; she allowed, and even encouraged, an exaggerated entertainment of his advances. Others noticed this as well.

The next day Ms Anders noticed that the mild repose upon her husband's face in the painting was melting into a pained and desperate expression. What was once a lofty, peaceful demeanor was slowly, daily, becoming an expression of sheer anguish. Guilt began to grip her very heart, as if even in death, she had offended his virtue.

Chanel's grief, still alive though submerged, actually surfaced in quarrels with her friends at school. Amazingly, to her, for we often feel that friendship has an eternal quality in it, she found that two of her closest friends simply were no longer 'there' for her. Chanel, in her youth had no way of measuring the impact that boys and girls had on one another at her tender age of fourteen.

She could sense a degradation occurring in her life. Of course we have the ever-present human capacity for dramatization, but, there was a sense of fatality in her feelings that she could not escape. Such feelings in youth are difficult to endure insofar as the entire emotional landscape is a constant tumult anyway.

She no longer visited the woodworking site of her father, which was actually a shrine for her, where she would reminisce for long periods on occasion. It was as if she had abandoned a temple.

Chanel had even heard the sound of wood saws at night...and in place of the formerly enthusiastic concentration and earnest work effort, the painting in her room portrayed a frantic, nearly maniacal aspect to the figure of her father in her painting. And, in time, he had clumsily dropped down upon one knee- as if the very supporting floorboards had been suddenly ripped from beneath him.

Soon, as days passed, the lumber stacked against the wall close to him became disorganized and threatened to tumble down across the room. The prized circular saw had fallen to the ground and appeared to have bent the blade. A most startling incident indeed! In life, his tools were endowed with the same care and austerity conferred to the best of friends.

Chanel did not see the change in exactly this way, but she did absorb the totality of the difference. She felt incredibly alone even though she was truly beyond the acute phase of her father's death: and still, things were not going well.

Blake was also witness to a material change in life, particularly through his relations with others.

Blake was a particularly adept point guard; but his teammates began to complain about his distribution of the ball. He actually tried desperately to understand and to compensate; after all, he prided himself on this part of his 'game', but to no avail. Finally, in a flurry of emotional fire he actually quit the team.

Blake had never quit anything in his life before.

One night, during this same period, Blake had heard the splashing of water, coming from seemingly nowhere, and everywhere. Upon examining the treasured painting the next morning, the figure of his father had begun to double over in the boat as if suffering enormous visceral pain. The fishing rod was surrendered to the lake, as well as one of the oars. Turbulence now exuded from the previously sedate pond, and dark clouds were gathering in the sky.

Impossibly, the paintings were changing of their own accord.

The changes, however, were only perceivable by their respective owner; usually on a midnight journey to the bathroom, or, awakening for no reason, far too early in the morning or returning far too late in the evening, only to be startled by the impossible. Whenever one of them attempted to bring it to the attention of another (if one could even remember witnessing a change), together, all they could witness of any of the paintings in question was the truly remarkable and affectionate force that conceived them.

In some deep closet of Ms. Anders mind there rumbled muffled guilt, but she had to do something. A professional detective would be at a complete loss here. Only a mother can sense this; they were no longer enveloped by Mr. Anders presence. The difficulties they experienced were not sinful in nature, they had more a character of simply being lost in the woods. And, there had to be a way to repair the ill wind pervading their lives.

Ms Anders instinctively recalled her original discussion with Ingram. The idea being sponsored by the absolute fixation he was known to be capable of, and the mortal dedication she heard in his voice when he pledged to produce a living depiction of Mr. Anders. Since Ms Anders, her children and Ingram dined together frequently she could no longer resist the compulsion to explore the phenomena she felt she had observed. The children concurred, and she asked Ingram if there was anything he could add to what was becoming a ghastly episode in their life in addition to their recent loss.

Ingram explained, as he himself slowly remembered, that he had in fact, used some of the ashes in all three paintings. Mrs. Anders felt her inner world quake, and every stable element in her mind disintegrated with this announcement. This was something Mrs. Anders had not expected. Ingram continued explaining how singular the entire experience was; he relayed the obsessive direction his efforts had taken. How the entire affair had an air of visitation surrounding it. Ingram continued with his effulgent descriptions until Ms Anders felt the need to grasp his hand, the same way you grab a child before crossing the street, instinctively surmising that this would keep this helium filled balloon earthbound.

Once she was convinced that Ingram was going to survive unscathed, she then resolved to attempt to repair the situation, with Ingram's consent, by burning the paintings, and returning the ashes to the dull brass urn from which they were garnered. The gravity of this decision was not lost on her. In a deeply burning fashion, she almost felt as if this was an incident amounting to a second cremation, tears were already streaming down her face; she also knew that it had become critical that she do something restorative, and the rising horror of paintings throughout her house that were changing of their own accord, and, possibly changing the lives of her family, which possessed them, left her no choice.

After performing the desperate act of destruction on the paintings, she completed her plan to restore the totality of the ashes to the urn.

That night, just before she retired, she noticed that the dull brass urn was visibly brighter; and smiling at her with the promise of a sunrise. She knew instantly that, even in death, she had restored the 'circle of concern' generated by Mr. Anders, simply through reuniting his ashes.

The End

By Hedy M. Gray, and Kenneth G. Gary

The Spring House Sale

By Kenneth G. Gary

Prelude

Are there no traces of our lives in the walls of our abode, in the tools we use, on the Earth we tread?

- A spiritual investigator.

Once Upon a Time...

The plane ride was smooth enough. The security lines had been short enough. The entire *'before your flight trauma'* had been mild enough. Why this intractable discomfort?

As Pilmer Holmes sat in his preferred window seat, exit row, looking out the window into total nighttime blackness, he relished the comfort of familiarity; this is the way he liked his flights. The window had that familiar duality where you could focus on the city lights below, or, adjusting your sight, you could see your own reflection in the window against the night.

Pilmer was flying from Texas back to Boston, where he was from. He was going to make the last adjustments regarding the sale of their property in Boston. His wife had managed most of the arrangements these past six months, but these last few arrangements had a portentous sense of finality to them. The house would be sold, its fate now in the hands of new owners, with new spirits, new habits, and new life. It actually left him mildly sad.

Approaching the house he stopped on the sidewalk to admire how grand it actually looked with the new white paint and gray trim. He remembered the summer he struggled with the perfectly straight chain linked fence surrounding the property. It only made separation more difficult.

The first thing to be done was to complete an exhaustive walk through; make sure that every item cited in the pending deal was in fact addressed.

He started in the basement.

He never really liked the basement. Well, he never felt completely comfortable in the basement, almost as if it belonged to someone else…

Yessss…this we know, and remember…

And this time was really no different. He checked the furnace; a huge converted coal burning iron monstrosity that now burned oil, creating steam that filled the radiators on the floors above. The huge 'arms' that carried the steam from its source to the upstairs radiators gave this system the image of a subterranean creature with tentacles that writhed throughout the entire building.

He checked the water level, the oil level, checked the whole system for leaks or any other anomaly that could be perceived. No apparent problems.

Having completed this check, but fully aware that he had not completed a check of the entire basement; Pilmer began his ascent up the stairway. Seldom do we admit the whispers we detect at the very edge of our being, and Pilmer, was quite satisfied to be climbing the stairs back into the familiar world that could be reached by the Sun.

Upstairs, while an improvement over the basement, it did not wash the traces of concern away completely. There was still a faintly persistent buzz, of some kind, not within the house, but deep within Pilmer himself.

Having conducted a cursory review of the premises, because, that is really all he could stand; Pilmer decided to prepare to go to the local restaurant for dinner. In the bathroom, *his* bathroom, he brushed his teeth, combed his hair, and in that last instant, where we always take an overview of our general appearance, turning our head right, now left; Pilmer saw with complete earth shattering horror that it was not *him* in the mirror at all: he was being *mimicked*!

As he turned to flee the bathroom, his soul was filled with screeching terror and unbelief at what he had just seen (had he screamed aloud?). What had he seen? Only *himself* in the mirror, but, unmistakably, the *reflection* was trying hard to imitate him without being detected!

The door slammed shut of its own volition, trapping him inside.

This gave Pilmer a freight that he first thought would just end his life. His heart pounded and his stomach turned – something within him even felt the floor move. But, in spite of limbs weak from fear, he managed to open the door and sprint into the dark hallway.

Amazingly, because the mind seems to surface concerns on its own schedule at times, the thought of planning to stay in this house for three days was already out of the question. How would he explain this to others? "Well, the house just did not want me in it..." right now, he did not care. He knew he had to get out before that *thing* in the mirror climbed out and...the conclusion was too horrific to imagine.

Pilmer nearly fell down the stairs, throwing open the door, and escaping to the outside, hoping that the insanity he just witnessed was somehow confined to *the house*.

Standing on the sidewalk, in the full brightness of a perfect summer day, he looked back upon the building that he just now noticed, had caused his entire body to sweat so that his suit clung to his arms and legs.

How do I proceed now? How do I show this house to prospects? How could I ever enter this abode again?

There is that seldom acknowledged phenomenon of things that can only happen when you are alone. Why is it that the shadow, which just pulled back from sight only does so when one is alone? The unmistakable footsteps, upstairs, when you *know* you are alone in the house; who makes them? We have all heard them, but no one knows...

We sssseee... and we will show thisssssss ...

Okay. The answer is to not be alone next time. I will only enter this house when it is time to show it to prospective buyers. Since I have to conclude this deal, this is how it will be done. After all, I cannot tell them it is haunted!

But, Pilmer could not deny those eyes! The mirror did not hold a reflection, but an attempt to *convince* him that it was a reflection. *And eyes show intent*. Pilmer could actually see that the reflection also understood that it had been discovered. Like a promise from some immortal source, this revelation attached a permanent grasp upon his heart; one he knew would never yield.

Even by mistake, the worst thing a human could ever do is witness the workings of the creatures of the night as they prepare, as they practice their ancient rituals, as they worship their eternal role of entrancing humans. They must then stalk and subdue you, so that you cannot reveal your discovery, their secrets…it is all about secrets! And the thing in the mirror had caught him looking through it's secret!

Okay, I will not go into the bathroom at all next time.

Pilmer finally met two lovely young ladies that seemed as innocent as the colorful leaves that blessed the New England countryside in autumn. Better yet, they were seriously interested in the house. If he had to guess, Pilmer thought the two young women, teachers, by all appearances, were very dedicated to their trade.

Though offering the 'salesman's smile', still, he could hear in the distant corners of his soul, an instrument that played in negative, discordant tones. Though it had not reached the surface of his consciousness, he was betraying himself, and these two young ladies, by showing them the house at all.

Soon he will be with ussss again…

The showing of the house was uneventful enough. Pilmer hoped not to evince any signs of how nervous, actually, terrified, he really was. The entirety of his sanity depended upon their very presence. He nearly revealed himself in the basement, where, they began to ascend the stairs as he was occupied with replacing several large boxes to their proper positions. Upon noticing that he was nearly alone in the cellar, his instincts propelled him, madly, towards the stairs nearly knocking his potential clients to the floor!

In their clear, sunshine begotten minds, by all appearances they mistook his insanity for mere haste, and patience prevailed. They did not really attend the incident at all. After all, it was rather dark.

Careful, lest he knowssss we are here…

Once back upstairs, where the late afternoon sun blessed the house through the windows, the two young teachers took those last, long looks at their surroundings, under the common misconception that they would be able to distinguish this house from several others they had visited that day. Pilmer, employed exemplary sales skills by his silence; not by design, but rather, because he hoped that no other anomaly would emerge to prolong his agony with this house.

Suddenly, with the speed of fright, the taller of the two women thrust a huge knife, gleaming in the afternoon sun, towards Pilmer's vital organs before he could respond. But, in reality, the young lady only offered her hand for a common handshake, which, after recovering from his vision, Pilmer accepted, and in fact returned, heartily. Fortunately, all this occurred within the speed of expanding eyes only.

Just then, the other woman mentioned the light that was left on in the kitchen, at the back of the house. Pilmer felt as though he had been delivered a death sentence in the highest court of the land! Yet, he could not reveal a perceivable sign of reluctance: He had to go to the back and turn off this ill begotten light! Any other behavior would raise questions about the consistency of maintenance.

Pilmer slowly, reluctantly walked back towards the kitchen. He felt like turning around and walking backwards to the kitchen, to make sure they did not go outside, leaving him alone in this house that was quickly becoming no more than a tomb. But that would leave him vulnerable to whatever was in the kitchen awaiting him. Forwards, backwards; there was no good answer.

He satisfied himself with frequent glances over his shoulder during what seemed to be a marathon progression from the front door, where they were, to the kitchen in the back of the house. On the way, there was an unmistakable 'bump' in an empty broom closet that he had to pass.

It is near impossible for a man to control his instincts: and for good reason; instincts have a more direct perception of certain phenomenon than cognition does. Cognition requires logic; instinct does not. The latter will save your life to figure things out later.

Nevertheless, Pilmer did jump, in a contained way, when he heard the sound.

Be sssstill, he is paying attention to us…Ashanti, Kamala…

Then he heard an even more ominous shuffling as something seemed to be moving away from the door, towards the back of the closet as he passed. *Of course, to escape my notice should I throw the door open. I am beginning to see what is going on here…* Pilmer said to himself with false bravado: He was consumed with the terror that he may not be able to return back past this door in order to leave this house! Ever!

All because of a light left on in the kitchen; *children, when your parents tell you to turn off lights, you really should do so.*

It was a straight line from the front of the house, where his young guests were waiting, down a long uninterrupted corridor to the kitchen where he had to address the delinquent light. But the kitchen, unlike the rooms towards the front of the house, had the stove, refrigerator and cabinets on the west wall – and no windows. So, when Pilmer turned off the kitchen light, as it was late in the day, the room was sent reeling into an abysmal darkness far beyond what could really occur in the middle of a sunny afternoon. It is still daytime! No, this darkness was born of some other, far more menacing origin…No sooner had he quenched the light than he heard one of the women from the front of the house "We will meet you outside. We want to take in the neighborhood!"

No more mortifying sentence could have been spoken to Pilmer at this time. Pilmer managed to not scream. He tried to answer and could not; only mist, like dry ice in water, issued forth from his mouth - *did I just hear them laughing as they left*?. In fact, he realized he was becoming surrounded by mist. The hallway to the front of the house looked to be a mile long. And there was the closet on the way…who knows what horror it barely held within.

There is that *moment* in life where, after applying the brakes, the car skids anyways, and quickly adjusting the wheel, the body simply braces itself for the inevitable impact…

Surely that impact was imminent. Strangely, there was a small measure of release in his stomach as Pilmer submitted to this understanding. But in the very next instant, the survival instinct immediately regained the wheel. All the sweat and tension returned – throwing off what was really a sedating effect of the thick mist that now snaked across the floor and up the walls of the kitchen.

Now Pilmer could see her.

With her head thrust back, arms stretched out sideways, mouth agape in clear agony, this woman, who seemed to be made of this mist, appeared in a far corner of the kitchen: In front of a large dark tree.

Pilmer was no longer in the kitchen at all.

Others, closed in around the lady of the mist, grabbing her, shoving her backwards into the tree behind her. Waving some of the ever increasing mist away from his face with his hands, Pilmer could make out, that it was not really a tree at all, but a very large 'container' of some kind, with a nearly human sized opening in it.

No sooner had she tumbled backwards through the door, with unmistakable terror on her face, Pilmer could see the inside of the container burst into ghastly flames.

Just like staring at a light source, then closing one's eyes: Pilmer could still see the silent scream written upon her face when she was - '*cast into Hell...*' - forced into the furnace... Why, that's it! What seemed to be a container was actually a large cast iron furnace. Not unlike the one in his basement?

At that very moment, the furnace in his basement had exploded, with the door flying open welcoming the escape of livid, hungry flames. With his consciousness barely emerging above the scene swirling around him, Pilmer turned his head to look down the hallway only to see the two young ladies, still as statues, until one of them raised her hand, bending her fingers solemnly several times to wave a fateful goodbye. The two turned and simply walked through the wall behind them.

It seemed the crowd before him in the mist had not noticed Pilmer standing behind them, and he wasted no more time. He glanced quickly left and right, only to find himself surrounded by a dense forest on both sides that was also invaded by the gossamer mist, which seemed to bubble and twist between the trees in a way that made it clear not to enter.

These sinsss belong to you.....

Gripped by a commanding fear, Pilmer spun around to take his chances and just run in the opposite direction from what had become a ghostly crowd in front of him who had also seemed to have chosen their next victim. As if from very far away, he could even hear the familiar, fervent, animal inspired rantings that people only make when they are in a crowd; the accusations that will acknowledge no explanations; the incriminations that entertain no defense.

Directly behind him, now face-to-face as he spun around, was the stark expression of death itself etched in the face of who he recognized to be the woman they had just thrown into the furnace.

As she gazed at him, her face changed. Her expression now wore the smooth countenance of certainty, of something being eternally finalized. He instinctively equated that with peace, in contrast with the anxious uncertainty that commonly rules our lives.

Instantly she grabbed him by the shoulders, his hopes of peace immediately evaporating, she was spinning him back around to face the scene at the furnace, and slowly forcing him forward to the very edge of the crowd, which still all had their backs to him. All except for the one standing next to the furnace addressing them.

Although he could not make out the words their leader spoke; that it was rhetoric and religious dogma, absent of all reason and light, was unmistakable. Pilmer was experiencing the essence of communication, that without which mere words do not matter anyway.

She violently grasped Pilmer by the hair from behind and forced him through the crowd into the front where he was, *once again*, face to face with this man, who, like a skillful musical conductor, elicited all the hate and fear necessary for them to commit their atrocities.

To his complete horror, Pilmer could see that this was the face from the mirror! It looked like him, but it was not a mere reflection, which, after all is what a mirror is supposed to offer.

Clearly, the man in front of his face could not even see him. None of them could, except this woman who had a superhuman grip on his body, forcing him in the direction of her intent.

Soon he will remember, and it will be finissshed…

And slowly Pilmer did remember. It was 1906, in a small town in New England. He, the vaunted Pilmer Westchester, had decided to resurrect the lifestyle of the Puritans. He felt strongly that their staunch regulation of life was all that was necessary to return man to the path of salvation. Pilmer, as has been common to most recorded religious historical figures, assumed that salvation could be secured on a scale that is wholesale.

Pilmer, with his outstanding sales abilities, influenced a small number of families to cohabitate in the woods outside the city limits. However, 'the best laid plans of mice and men', while documented in fiction, is an eternal human reality; things took on a far more fervent tone than Pilmer ever anticipated, even from himself.

The two young girls that were finally openly charged with witchcraft, after having long been suspected of lesbianism, were taken into 'custody' by the mob one night. That was the scene that Pilmer was witnessing in his 'Kitchen'. Needless to say, the girls were not witches, although they were lesbians. It was in fact the Puritans insult with the latter that lead to the formulation of the former. Pilmer had actually always known the truth, but refused to look at this simple fact. He only fanned the flames.

Now Pilmer was recalling everything. The ghost woman behind him even released her grasp; she too knew that his fate had finally caught up with him. He no longer struggled, he knew the inescapable nature of what was unfolding.

Pilmer was doubly damned by the fact that he did know real witches, with whom he had conspired to sacrifice these two girls, in order to allay suspicions in the true direction of the eternal evil that did exist. And this in return for the promise of lasting influence over the commune he had collected.

An essential part of his deal with the witches was that should he return to life again, reincarnated, he would never have a memory, nor dream, nor suspicion about the crimes he was committing on their behalf. They had agreed.

His escape was well designed: If you cannot remember, you really are not hiding at all. It in fact did not even occur as far as you know. How could Pilmer ever suspect that he would walk the earth again in close proximity to a simple, inanimate instrument of torture that absorbed the agony all unto itself. How could Pilmer ever suspect that the innocent girls he condemned could possibly leave a 'residue' within the iron chamber? So strong as to resurface and wreak their revenge?

The furnace ...was silent witness to the entire atrocity. And, after all; the witches told him he himself would not remember; they did not promise him he could not be made to remember by others.

With the inevitability of the setting sun, Pilmer was already walking towards the furnace himself. The flames within were not so much damaging to the flesh as they were searing to the soul. The two ladies within the flames beckoned him with outstretched arms. Pilmer was beginning to know the abysmal pain that was his fate in every life he would ever lead.

And so it would seem that, if not the mundane in our existence, at least the extraordinary is etched into whatever surroundings exist at the time.

One Blue Mitten

By Hedy M. Gray

The old lady breathed an unseen deep, heavy sigh. She was resigned to her fate. The monitor levels shot up a bit, then settled back down. There were no other signs of life except the dull monotonous hum of the pumps. There was no one there to see her except the bright eyes of the monitors.

Oh no, she thought. Here they come again. Why can't they just leave me alone? I'm tired, so tired... it's been so long... too long. I wish I were a bird, then I would flap my wings and just fly away. Nothing's any good any more. But sometimes I remember when it was good. I remember... sensations... tastes... feelings... Sometimes I dream of just a cool drink of water going down my throat... the feel... Or I wish for a piece of bread... a cracker. I can almost feel it crossing my tongue... melting in my mouth. Ummmmm... I almost remember the taste... the feel... the smell... almost.

But it's been a long time now. They think I'm blind but, I see and I don't even have to look. I can feel the room slowly begin to lighten or darken. There are so many shades of darkness and light and I am familiar with each and every one of them. There are many different sounds of silence, too and I've heard them all.

Now this silence is broken, I hear the door open. I hear a dim light flicked on. I hear quiet, quick footsteps. I listen as they make three brief stops and now I know there are four of us here. I can hear their machines pumping, pumping, pumping like an orchestra of low, bass instruments. It's an irritating sound... The steps stop at my station. No talking, shh, don't wake the dead. I listen. I hear everything: the wind, the silence, the footsteps, the soft voices.. The hysterical weeping of the others, their pleadings... just like mine.

I've been here so long. Others have come and gone. I'm still here. Months?... years?... a decade or two?... Doesn't really matter, seems like forever... it is forever because I can't remember any time before now. Time means nothing. Nothing means anything... there's only my yearning to be free.. A constant all-consuming want.

I don't know what crime I committed to be put here in ... this prison... on death row. Waiting, always waiting... I wish to God it was over but, every time, when I'm just about to be let go... un-plugged... executed... released... set free... Freedom! How I pray... wish for it... But there's no escape from this prison. Each time I think I'm about to be pardoned... paroled... released, whatever... some good-for-nothing, holy right-to-lifer- special interest group sticks their nose in my business and I'm given more time on this... death row. I think it's been years and years now and I'm more than ready to go. But I got life without parole, didn't I? I'm ready, have been ready for eons... Oh, just kill me please!

Jannie got up and gently woke David from his nap, "sweetie pie, we can't sleep all day. We have important things to do."

A sleepy child tried to smile hearing there was something 'potant to do, "what 'potant thing, Momma?"

"First, look here, I have something for you," his mother said handing him a small bag.

"What is it?" the now fully awake child cried as he tore excitedly into the bag ignoring the happy wintery scene printed on the front.

One small pair of new, warm, blue mittens fell out of the bag and onto his bed. The child screamed, "oh goody!"

"Now, be very careful. Don't lose these like you did the red ones. It's very cold outside and remember you can't go out without mittens," his mother warned lovingly.

David loved to be outside, but last week he had been held prisoner in the house just because of the loss of one red mitten. He didn't know where or even when he had lost it. "I will not let these new blue mittens get lost!" he vowed trying on the new mittens.

At first I didn't want to meet the end, I struggled... fought tooth and nail to wake up and live. Then eventually I come to grips with the inevitability of it all. I got tired. Stopped fighting. Death became an old friend waiting for me just around the corner. I saw him, but can't quite make the turn, death was always just out of my reach. There were a few times when I felt myself almost touching deaths outstretched hand only to be yanked back by some drug or machine.

They're here again, I can hear them, see them even anticipate their actions. I promised myself that I would try one more time to make contact... to move my eyes, my mouth a finger a foot... anything to let them know the answer to the question never asked of me. I want them to know my answer. Not the answer they assume they get from me. The answer they want to see... to hear. They decide what I want. I am not allowed to have an opinion about me!

They can walk around, move, laugh, cry, feel, smell, touch... I can no longer do any of this. They love life because they have it. They assume I love life, too. I did when I had it... This is not life.

"Are you comfortable?" they ask looking in my face not seeing me.

HELL NO!!! It's too hot and I want to lay on my right side.

"She's probably cold, turn the heat up a little. There! Her eyes are moving up and down now. Yes, that's what she wanted."

YOU IDIOT!!! My eyes were going sideways until you tried to scorch my skin! NO! I'm saying no! Look at me not that damn monitor, it lies! Oh! You make me so sick! I hate you all! Why can't you just let me go!? I'm ready, been ready for years.

"Ops, I'll put the covers back. Did you see that? She kicked the covers off as a thank you. She can hear us!" one of the idiots say.

Yes I can hear you, you fool, but you can't hear me! You refuse to listen, look... just try. Think about it, would you like to be lingering on with one foot here and the other poised at the door to freedom... if this is my eternity... do I deserve it? Would you like to live this way? LIVE?! This sure as hell ain't living.

Oh, they're bringing in another poor soul. Two left yesterday, but not me. I'm the Grand ole lady here. They just keep pumping me up and watching the machine. I have all the bells and whistles of a Frankenstein's lab. What; is this the way they get their jollies? Torturing poor helpless souls? I'm ready to go now! Just please let me go!

Oh no! There's another smiling face. What does it want? Okay I'll gather all my strength again and try to talk... to move... I'm ready. Just ask me. I'm ready, I'm ready, I'm ready... Take a deep breath, let it out slowly. Calm down. Watch them. Are they watching me? Please watch me! Look! Look at me! Yes!

Here I go. "Kill me please. Did you hear that? No, he's not looking any more. He's enraptured by that damn monitor. Now he's looking again. Kill me please.

"How are we today?" the smiling face asks looking at my machines.

We? How do you think?

"Are you feeling better?"

Of course, want to change places?

One finger, move one finger. There I did it! Oh, damn he's not looking again.

"There now," he said patting me then he wiped the sweat off my face.

Don't touch me!

"We're very agitated today aren't we? What can I do for you?"

Let me die..

"... Your granddaughter and her son are here to see you again. Maybe they'll read a little to you. Why don't you ask 'em?"

Very funny!

"Hi Grammie, it's me, Jannie and David." Jannie said looking upbeat and trying to smile through a hidden cry.

Fool, I know who you are.

"David, do you want to kiss Grammie?"

"No," a sullen child whispered under his breath.

Hell no I wouldn't even want to kiss me. Leave the child alone.

"Oh David see you made Grammie cry. She wants a kiss."

"She looks bad. I ain't gonna kiss her!"

Atta boy David don't let nobody make you do it.

"Do you want us to read to you Grammie?"

No.

"Oh look David Grammie's smiling, yes."

No I'm not, it's a frown. Get that child outta here! Can't you see I'm frightening him?

"Okay. We'll read one David likes, The Little Train That Could. Come on David help me read to Grammie.

Read one flew over the coo coos nest. Kill me please.

"Momma Grammie said something."

"No she didn't. She's just breathing hard. She can't talk."

"Yes she can Momma, I heared her."

"Well then, what did she say?"

"I don't know."

"Be quiet and listen to the story."

Kill me please David tell them to Pull the plug.

"Where Grammie?"

"David, listen to the story and be quiet!"

"Ma'am? We hate to interrupt you but it's time to take some test. Please excuse us. You can come back after a bit."

"It's okay we were just about to leave anyway. Come on David help me get everything together."

"Bye Grammie. Sorry I can't kiss you," David whispered.

It's okay baby boy. There, that was a smile.

"Look Momma, Grammie smiled!"

Kill me please.

"She said it again, 'feel my knees'! That's what she said Momma." a joyful David said happy he was able to hear his Grammie better this time.

"Okay, let's go David. Bye Grammie. See you again next week," Jannie said as she brushed near her cheek.

NEXT WEEK! Hope I'm dead by then. kill me please.

"She okay? Her facial expressions are... strange..." Jannie observed.

"She's okay... just been a little agitated today this'll calm her down," the doctor said while holding a needle up in the light.

NO! Don't give me a shot! I don't want to be calm, I want to be dead. PULL THE PLUG!! I can roll my eyes and roll my head. Jannie, don't go! Pull the plug, please. I'm ready to go.

"What's wrong? Is she reacting to my leaving?" Jannie asked hopefully. "Did she feel the shot? Did it hurt?"

"No, she can't feel anything,"

How do you know? Are you in my skin?

"... she sometimes gets a little agitated when there's any change. I just pulled the shade, it's darker in here now. She'll be all right."

No. I won't be all right. kill me please. I have a right to die. The real me is sitting over here in this chair watching, but nobody sees me. You're too busy watching that dead, empty monster in the bed.

Who's that? David. What's he doing? Feeling my knees! I love you baby boy. KILL... ME... PLEASE! PULL THE ... PLUG!

The small boy barely touched her knee before he was pulled out the door by his rushing mother.

"Won't you please come with us this time?" Jannie begged her husband.

"No. You know I don't agree with what you're doing," he said standing in the kitchen doorway.

"What am I supposed to do, kill her?"

"She's already dead."

"You don't know that!" Jannie yelled. "I wish Momma was here, she'd know what to do," Jannie moaned.

"Yeah, she'd find a way to get the insurance money for herself..."

"Why do you hate my family?"

"I thought David and I where your family..." he stated in a hurt voice.

"You are... but... Grammie is all I have left of the old..."

"All this... it's costing..." he interrupted.

"It's not costing us a thing... The insurance..."

"And the state..."

"It's not costing you one red cent...!"

"Not money, but there's other cost..."

"Shh, here comes David. Hi baby! ready to go?"

"I can't find my gloves," David said searching franticly in his coat pockets.

"Look in here," his mother said tossing him his hat.

Sure enough tucked neatly inside the hat were the red mittens. Right where his mother had put them.

David grinned relieved and prepared to leave the house. He made a little snow ball as he walked to the car. He stomped in snow drifts and tried to taste the snow that fell in his open mouth. He felt free outside in the open.

The visit to Grammie was normal. She just lay there. Jannie read and had to pull David away from the equipment on the other side of her bed, twice.

"David! You stay over here... away from all the equipment."

"Why?" David whined looking at all the inviting wires and cords leading to Grammie in the bed.

"It helps Grammie to breathe and if a cord is moved she can't breathe," Jannie explained, again for the umpteenth time.

"David!! Where are you?" Jannie yelled when it was time to go.

David was almost asleep on the floor at the foot of the bed.

David jumped up and hurriedly grabbing his gloves he ran toward the door.

Tell them to pull the plug. I want to be dead.

He stopped short and looked around, "I don't see it, Grammie."

His mother appeared in the door and yelled, "David, come on now!"

"Momma there's a bug in Grammie's room."

"I'll tell the orderly, come on," his mother insisted pulling David out the door.

That week was like a decade as she lay alone in her bed. Someone would come in early each day and mark the calendar. Another day gone. Slowly the window went from dark to light, to dark again to light again. Over and over again the same routine: Mark the calendar, turn her, give her a shot, mark down everything... verify her life, change her, wash her, fill the feeding tubes, turn her, pull the shades...

"Hi Grammie," a smiling Jannie said. "How are we today?"

We are the same today as we were yesterday and the day before that. Waiting, wishing to die. How are you? Does it feel good to walk around? Where's David?

"I can't stay long, I have to pick David up from a birthday party. It's just you and me today. Can I get you anything?"

Yes, pull the plug. Let me go.

"Are you warm enough?"

Does it matter?

"I know David's sad to have missed coming today, here's a kiss from him."

Yeah right, you missed my cheek by inches. You don't even want to kiss me why, in hell do you try to force that baby to kiss me?

"How is she doing, doctor?"

Why don't you ask me? How do you think I'm doing? Wanting, wishing, praying to be dead.

"As well as can be expected. Where's the child? She seems to brighten up when he comes."

"He had a birthday party to go to."

"Mister man-on-the-town?" the doctor teased.

"Yeah, he is at that age when parties are so important," Jannie smiled.

I thought you came to see me. Talk to me. Tell me what's going on in the world. Since you took out the TV and changed the radio to elevator music I have no idea what's going on. You said it was better for me. How!? Oh yeah, I forgot. I need to be kept quiet, no agitation...

"Why do you want to keep her plugged in?" the doctor asked, again.

"She's my Grandmother. It will be like killing her, I can't do that," Jannie moaned softly.

"Don't think about it like that. She's in a coma. After this long her brain activity is almost nil... very low. She will never be the same even when or if she comes out of the coma. You won't be killing her, you'll be letting her rest. Putting her at peace."

Exactly. I'll be at rest. Finally. Let me rest, let me go, please.

"I can't do this! I've got to go... get my son," Jannie said rushing out of the room.

Another week of loneliness, hopelessness... Mark off the days, repositioning, watching the monitors, pulling the shades, watching the window grow light then dark. Another eternity.

"Good morning! Look who I have here. David came," a cheery Jannie said as she walked into the room.

Oh good my baby boy came. Just don't make him kiss me, please.

"Say hi to Grammie, David."

"Hi Grammie."

Hi David, tell them today, let me go, pull the plug. see the plug? pull it.

"Grammie wants to go to the baffroom but she sees a bug," David said

"David, I made sure there were no bugs in the room. Now you just stop. She can't go to the bathroom. Now sit down and help me read to her."

"Hi, good to see you brought the little boy. She'll be happy to see him," the doctor said.

"Don't talk to me about pulling the plug today, ok?" Jannie said.

"You know about the bug?" David asked in wonderment.

"The bug? What bug?"

"Grammie tells me about pulling the bug," David said.

"What? What does your Grammie say?"

"Feel my knees and pull the b... plug," David said remembering the hard word.

"He gets his Bs, Ps and sometimes Ds mixed up sometimes," Jannie explained.

"Does your Grammie talk to you?" the doctor asked.

David started fidgeting and held on to his mother and hid his face in her lap.

"It's OK baby answer the doctor, all right."

"Yes... She talks to me," David admitted hesitantly.

"Tell me when she talks to you the next time, OK?" Jannie said.

"Yes ma'am," David promised.

"Don't talk about, you know. The child must of heard us," Jannie said to the doctor.

On the way down the hall to the elevator, David and Jannie were passed by a swarm of hospital personnel all clad in white, rushing down the corridor, pulling beds on wheels, dragging IV stands and an assortment of other equipment. There was obviously some sort of emergency...

As they were getting on the elevator, David shoved his hands into his coat pocket. He immediately noticed with alarm that one red mitten was gone!

Quickly he ducked down between all the legs and slipped through just before the elevator doors closed. He heard his Momma yell his name and he shouted back, "I lost my mitten...!"

David ran back down the hall, past the empty nurse's desk and into Grammie's room. Grammie looked the same. Nervously he began to talk to her as he scanned the floor near her bed where he expected to find the mitten.

"Grammie I lost my mitten. Do you know where it is? I can't go out to play without it..." He thought she said look on the floor.

He looked. It was not there.

David is that you? I'm tired. Tell 'em to pull the plug, please. I'd rather be dead, I don't want to see another day. Kill me please..

He squeezed Grammie's knees then got down and peered under the bed. There! On the bad side of the bed near the wires lay his mitten.

"Thank you Grammie, I see it," he said as he ducked under the bed, pass the beeping machine being very careful not to disturb any of the wires or cords. He grabbed his blue mitten and being very careful not to hit his head on the way out he scooted back under the bed to the other side.

He smiled at Grammie and squeezed her knees again, "thank you, Grammie." David hesitated one moment more. Then he gave Grammie a butterfly kiss on her gnarled hand.

Unbeknown to him, the little boy's foot pulled one very important cord ever so slightly.

"God Bless you child. Tell your mother good bye." And Grammie smiled.

"OK Grammie," he said as he squeezed his grandmother's knees one more time on his way out the door.

"Where were you?" Jannie asked as she met David in the hall..

"Grammie said good bye," David said sure at last what his Grammie said.

Late that night a wind blew through the halls of the hospital and the plug, already barely in wall contact, wiggled the rest of the way out of the wall. Grammie sank her head back deep into the pillow. She was definitely smiling the next morning when the nurse came in to check on her.

They notified the next of kin later that day.

The Halloween Chase

By Kenneth G. Gary

Prelude

Even a thickly populated market is not a haven…not when the world changes.

Once upon a time…

Parents never really tell you much, and you never really know what questions to ask, but I think that my father was promoted to a position that allowed, or perhaps demanded, that we move to another more distant part of the city.

New schools are never comfortable. The cliques are already well formed and you are a nomadic beast that does not belong to any of the several prides.

In time, through the many normal interactions of youth, I emerged with a couple of friends. One was just a bit boisterous; the other was far more ruminating in nature. It was a strange combination but they both shared one quality that most people value highly in friendship; their behavior did not alter depending on the social environment. Neither an opportunity for social advancement, nor the prospect of a beautiful girl, altered the way that we treated one another. We had fallen upon a distinctly complimentary chemistry.

That fall the beginning of the school year passed quickly and our friendship grew into that comfortable fauna for which there is no name; it is only recognized by its character.

Within a month we were well acquainted.

Autumn, with a stunning display of color, became far more comfortable, and soon, my favorite holiday was upon us. It was a Halloween of great expectation, the first for me in this new area of town, and, the prospect of sharing it with my newfound friends heightened the importance.

The week preceding Halloween, my mother, who was at no loss for enjoyment of frightful activities, had taken me to the local 'circus' (state fair really, this reference was born of my disdain). Twice. Bored with clowns and other childish foolishness – *why do parents never realize how old we really are?* – I finally stumbled upon a crowd. They exuded 'oooh's and 'aaaah's with such rapture I could not help but investigate. I squeezed my way to the front of the crowd.

There was a rather tall, majestic and theatrical magician on stage wearing a long black coat with tails and a tall stovepipe cylindrical hat. He had two assistants, who stoically positioned themselves at either side of the stage, and, there was a woman who escapes all attempts at description of her beauty, serving as his assistant. Though I did not recall many specifics of the performance, I knew I had visited a magic show; A real one. The acts performed by this magician were absolutely not possible. And it appeared to me that the one constant among all his feats was his wand, which somehow enabled these unbelievable magical tricks.

He performed the perfunctory sawing of the lady in half, enclosing her in a casket of fatally sharp knives, and so on. But, there was something about the minor feats performed that were not actually part of the act but more sheer exuberance that poured out without being scripted at all; it was the music that is played between the 'sets'; unscheduled.

I watched as after the lady emerged from one of her death defying confinements, the tall man wrapped one arm around her waist and raised the wand high in the air with the other hand. I noticed that she secured their bond by wrapping one arm around him also, in anticipation, with the other arm high in the air in recognition of the rising applause. Suddenly, they both began to sprint across the stage, towards the audience, and leap up into the air with their momentum supporting them until they were nearly horizontal in the air high above the heads of the crowd. As if on a swing, they were gently returned to the middle rear of the stage from whence they had begun.

In itself such a feat could be easily explained away with wires and other such contraptions that could be employed to support the illusion. There was something about the arc of their flight, and the uneven traversal of the distance that belied any such theory. Even a child can judge the arc and position of a fly baseball in the outfield; and there was something unnatural about the way they were able to 'fly' above the heads of the crowd, in an unpredictable arc, and return to the stage so gently.

The final measure, however, was the fact that it was an outdoor stage with no ceiling capable of supporting what would be necessary wires for support.

At the end of another feat I know that I saw the tall man glide to the front of the stage without walking. That is to say that the two or three paces he did exert in no way account for the distance he covered. And, again, all the while he held the sparkling black, silver tipped wand above his head.

There was something, if not real magic, at least it was extraordinarily odd at work here. My suspicion was inflated by the fact that their clear goal was to perform the commonly expected 'magic routines' while they could not seem to suppress the expression of some genuine power that was barely contained. The applause of the audience seemed to accentuate this expression between every act.

On the late afternoon preparation of Halloweens expected adventures, I anxiously relayed to my two friends how I had witnessed actual magic! They listened, uninterested, but I continued my presentation until finally Billy, the boisterous one, said 'Okay, let's settle this. We'll all go and see'. This is exactly what I wanted, and we proceeded to the fairground.

Again, the magician's stage was assailed by an enraptured audience that freely exulted in the absolute wonder of his skill. And he, with every nuance of showmanship, strode about the stage magnetically garnering the crowd's attention, and stoking their wonder. Surreptitiously, we positioned ourselves at strategic corners of the stage. We planned to determine once and for all what was possibly taking place here.

Being children, our attention span wandered. Billy and me had just finished our large drinks and tossed ice cubes across the distance at one another. I knocked my oversized ice filled cup over during the activity. It was sitting on the stage and the ice cubes scattered over the stage surface near me.

There was one moment of opportunity, where he laid his wand in the middle of the stage, and, since no wooden surface regularly exposed to the outdoors remains perfectly flat, it innocently rolled towards me. The wand easily passed the ice cubes on the stage but the magician, who had vigorously pursued it, came to a frozen halt upon encountering the ice cubes. He actually looked frightened, and his movement was no longer graceful but rather ungainly. Without thinking at all, inspired by some unnamed impulse; I grabbed it. I turned and we ran as fast as we could, darting and ducking through the crowd. Looking back over my shoulder I could see that he immediately sensed the crime, and his eyes; his eyes held a preternatural gleam that would have apprised a more mature person of the ensuing disaster thus incurred. But we were children, and all things were possible to us. I shoved the wand, only a foot in length, into the inner pocket of my jacket; on the left side, next to my heart and ran as fast as the immediate crowd would allow.

Deftly navigating our way through the crowded fair grounds, a sideward glance revealed a ghastly image of a tall shadow, wearing a tall top hat that appeared to move across the tents and food wagons, in our direction, as we hastily secured our escape. In full stride, I could not help but notice, or rather; my mind could not help but register, the way that a shadow becomes bent and acutely angular as it passes over the physically disparate surfaces upon which it is cast.

Having covered the distance from the fairgrounds proper to the more commercial territory of the town (as the fair was held at 'City Center'), there was a brief moment when the shadow could not be detected on the nearby walls and roofs of the shops and stores we passed. Being an old, urban section of town we were afforded the opportunity to quickly duck into an abandoned bodega, with the intent of examining our prize.

No sooner had I begun to unzip my jacket we saw through a broken out window the shadow again. It was cast upon the wall and across the roof of a two-story building directly across the street. This vision immediately implied huge proportions to the owner of said shadow. But, there was something wrong, or out of place. The shadow cast on the buildings across the street would have to be produced by an owner – which should be directly in front of us out this window also (since the sun late in the day, was to our backs at this point).

But there was nothing there.

Moreover, there was something wrong with the shadow itself. Sensibly, though outrageous in terms of proportions, the outline of the legs climbed up to the second story of the building across the street, whereupon, the torso seemed to lay across the 45-degree angular roof. But, the roof, not being of sufficient length to support the entirety of this menacing shadow, the head and shoulders were cast above the apex of the roof, against – nothing!

A shadow requires a background upon which to be cast, and this one, with the expanse of the roof being exhausted, was simply cast vertically in the air against, nothing.

Without speaking, we darted from the abandoned structure and continued to flee in the direction opposite of the fair grounds. There was a distinct warmth emanating from the (stolen) wand in my inside jacket pocket. It also seemed to be pressing tighter against my rib cage. Even at a young age, it was clear to me this was the surfacing of a guilty conscious manifesting in these symptoms.

This vastly oversized shadow, with no perceivable source, easily kept close pace with us as we ran. In fact, it seemed to grow in stature, shifting our escape into frightful proportions. And then, it began, at least as far as I can recall, with a change in the wind. It had a certain gravity to it. It was not a hurricane or storm of any kind, nothing energetic; just a slow, thickly palpable wind, more like liquid than air; and capable of moving everything in existence - which had become unstable. It seemed to have waited centuries for this very occasion where this was possible.

The magnitude and pervasive nature of this 'change' scattered our senses and our paths lost all unison. We were running in different directions and confusion ensued.

In time, however, we reconvened at one of those super shopping marts, our predetermined rendezvous. With the attending atmospheric changes there was also that huge shadow again that stalked along the walls of the grocery mart. Our previous plans to seek the secrets of the wand evaporated as the phantasmagoric effects surrounding us increased. We quickly decided to split up and pursue different directions, and, I was entrusted to safeguard the wand. No sooner had my friends vanished than I noticed what risk our decision bode, especially for me, as it is undoubtedly the wand he is after – for he is certainly here!

I thought first that I would simply pull the wand out and drop it in full view. I expected he would find it. But it would not budge from my pocket. Neither could I remove the jacket from myself as the wand was somehow adhering to my rib cage.

The air itself coalesced into a thick mire, and of the people that I could see, they were all moving slower and slower, until they were perfectly still, in whatever ungainly posture they were caught in at the moment. Then, very slowly, they began to move again. But there was something positively wrong about this movement, and it took several moments to see what the problem was.

They were all moving backwards. Carts were coming in from the parking lot, people were re-entering the checkout line from the departure side, putting groceries back on the counter. People were walking backwards. And that was his way of knowing who you were; by contrast with everyone else. Time was being re-wound. Now this is totally unlike time travel into the past, where upon arrival, time continues its 'normal' direction. No, it was being un-wound, set on reverse, unraveling.

As people opened up their car trunks, to remove the grocery bags, place them back in the carriages to re-enter the store, his steady, monstrous stride, continued down Main Street.. Seeking his victim from amongst the sleeping sheep...for this was his way of 'parting the waters'; by putting everything in reverse, since people cannot remember things backwards (otherwise you could remember the future), he could walk (stalk?) amongst us and consume victims at will.

He already knew the general proximity of our destination was the super store on Campbell Road. Clothed in flowing, black leather garments, head adorned with an equally protective tall leather hat, he glared with eyes that shone like lions in the night. And my heart was gripped with terror that his eyes would fall upon me with recognition. My heart could already feel that I was on the radar somehow.

Suddenly my mind seized upon an answer: Simply blend in! Could I not also walk backwards, retrieve money from the cashier and proceed to replace items upon the very shelves from which they were gathered?

This strategy will protect me from detection. His effort at turning the whole world around in order to identify me will then be in vain. I will simply back my way out of this environment right in front of him in the different time stream of his own creation...

Then I noticed another boy. Tall, thin, pale and utterly stricken with freight. Our momentary glance conveyed the abysmal terror we shared. He was visibly shaking, and I, in my complete concern with self-preservation, felt myself to be more secure in the fact that I would not be the first victim at least. This kid is sweating liquid fear. It has to be a signpost, a target for a heat-seeking missile that will at least buy me some time.

I wondered how long this other child had been 'here', between worlds; because this was not the world I had been born in. Then I noticed something critical. The other kid was looking over his shoulder as he moved backwards; but no one else was. They were all swept up in a genuine reversal of time, unconscious and involuntary.

Their steps were simply the rewind from a movie, but this kid I saw, was going to reveal himself because he, and I, were not 'one' with the fabric of this reversal. Looking over his shoulder as he walked backwards was going to single him out, beckoning his doom.

Out of sheer terror, I grasped the handle of a shopping cart. The woman who had used it originally, returned, walking backwards. She grabbed the handle without noticing me, emptied the contents of her trunk back into the cart, and began her backwards progress to the cavernous super store. Occasionally, she looked left and right for parking lot traffic, as she must have done on the original path out of the store, and she had no perception whatsoever that I was there, though both of us manned the cart; she simply looked right through me.

Fortunately this woman was old enough to be my mother, and, if I simply relinquished my will, and keeping my grip on the handle, followed her and the cart, it would guide my path backwards into the store without my looking over my shoulder to see where I was going. This guise may just save my life.

Once the lady and I were in the store, he just crashed right through the glass doors. And, this was not the haunting shadow that had pursued me; it was he in the flesh. I panicked, and was discovered immediately. With my ruse completely abandoned, I simply fled down the nearest aisle, darting between people who could not see me. He pursued at a rapid but relaxed pace. At the end of the aisle, I turned the corner, and with no other option I ran down the aisle with misting fresh vegetables on one side and exposed frozen foods on the other.

Wheeling around to measure the progress of his predation, I was astounded to find that he came to a complete halt at the entrance to this aisle. He took one trembling step forward, and then retreated. He just stood there, quaking with intent, until finally he raised his fists skyward, and throwing his head back, there erupted a terrifying silent scream.

He was unable to enter the frozen food section. Then I remembered the ice cubes I had spilled on the stage and how they had brought him to a complete halt.

I felt my jacket relax; the wand fell innocently to the floor and rolled intently, almost affectionately, down the aisle to its proper owner. It was a brilliant sky blue. He knelt down and with both hands caressed the wand upon its arrival, stood up, gave me a searching glance (and nearly a sardonic smile) and turned and walked away.

You see, the wand was powerful and mischievous, and had not enjoyed a good game in a long while.

ABOUT THE AUTHOR

Kenneth G. Gary was born in Atchison, Kansas, grew up in Minneapolis, Minnesota, and moved to Boston, Massachusetts, where he earned a degree in Biological Anthropology at Harvard University. He now works internationally as an IT architect and lives in Dallas, Texas.

Hedy M. Gray was born in Atchison, Kansas. She grew up in Minneapolis, Minn. She was married and has three grown children and fine grandchildren. She went to college in Iowa and majored in Journalism. Hedy has been writing for quite some time. Her first published writing was a short piece for her school newspaper about some stairs that went nowhere. She is a PushCart award nominee (December 2015).

Printed in the United States
By Bookmasters

Printed in the United States
By Bookmasters